Sherlock Holmes & THE ULTIMATE DISGUISE

"... last address was Toronto, Ontario ..."
(King Street West)

Sherlock Holmes & THE ULTIMATE DISGUISE

from the Annals of John H. Watson, M.D.

Ronald C. Weyman

⊞ Simon & Pierre
Toronto, Canada

We would like to express our gratitude to the Canada Council and the Ontario Arts Council for their support.

Marian M. Wilson, Publisher

Illustrations: Buffalo and Erie County Historical Society, 120; Canadian Pacific Archives, 18, 23; McCord Museum of Canadian History, 75; Metropolitan Toronto Library Board, frontispiece, 54, 84, cover; Francis Petrie Estate, 106, 132; cover illustration by Mr. Melton Prior for *The Illustrated London News*, Dec. 15, 1888: "Interior of a Colonial Sleeping Car on the Canadian Pacific Railway."

ISBN 0-88924-232-1

1 2 3 4 5 • 6 5 4 3 2

Canadian Cataloguing in Publication Data

    Weyman, Ronald C., 1915-
        The ultimate disguise.

    ISBN 0-88924-232-1

I. Title.

PS8595.E85U5 1991   C813'.54   C91-094927-1
PR9199.3.W48U5 1991

General Editor: Marian Wilson
Editor: Jean Paton
Design: C.P. Wilson Graphic Communication
Printer: Marc Veilleux Inc.
Printed and Bound in Canada

Order from
Simon & Pierre Publishing Company Limited / Les Éditions Simon & Pierre Ltée.
P.O. Box 280 Adelaide Street Postal Station
Toronto, Ontario, Canada M5C 2J4

Contents

Illustrations

Acknowledgements

With great respect to Sir Arthur Conan Doyle.
To my dear wife Vanna.

Foreword

In the year 1892, my good friend Sherlock Holmes and I joined forces in the peculiar case which came to be known as "The Mark of the Beast."

Under instructions from no less a personage than His Royal Highness "Bertie," Prince of Wales, heir to the British throne, we had participated in the demonstration of a newly-devised instrument of naval warfare — the "submarine." In the process, we were also fortunate enough to divert a particularly foul plot to assassinate His Royal Highness, an event which, if successful, would have changed the course of world history.

As I have set out elsewhere, the disappearance and presumed demise of Holmes in the fearful cataract of the Reichenbach Falls on May 8th, 1891 — an event duly reported by the London newspapers — was in fact a ruse, deliberately planned at the highest levels of the British Government, to allow him to go underground on this, perhaps the most important mission of his career.

A master of concealment, the great detective assumed the ultimate disguise — the appearance of his own death — as, locked in the arms of his arch-enemy Professor Moriarty, he plunged over the Reichenbach Falls into the frightful abyss below, and in that dreadful cauldron of swirling water was lost to human ken.

Holmes, however, his escape route planned, made his way incognito to Montpellier in the south of France, where a well-equipped laboratory was at his disposal. To meet the urgent needs of Her Majesty's Government, Holmes was to conduct research into the coal-tar derivatives, in truth nothing less than the historic development of a "smokeless gunpowder," destined in those politically uneasy times to maintain Britain in the forefront of world powers.

The newly perfected explosive coincided with, and indeed made possible, a new and frightful range of weaponry which was applauded by Her Majesty's Government, at a time when Germany was planning a Grand Fleet to challenge Britain's supremacy at sea, the Boers were in conflict in South Africa, and the Russians were pressing at the gates of India.

My account of the affair was not published at the time, touching as it did on the secret development of powerful engines of war, destined to shape world history. Of even greater concern in some circles, and therefore deemed even less suitable for publication, were my delicately phrased references to some aspects of the private life of our esteemed Prince of Wales, and indeed of the father of our revered Queen Victoria herself. I had not sought notoriety in these observations, but they seemed pertinent to my account, and essential elements of my report, despite Holmes, who on occasion accused me of indulging in sensationalism.

Suffice it to say that the extraordinary events of this *cause célèbre* landed me finally, exhausted, far from the familiar streets of London, in the noble Canadian citadel of Quebec, feeling older even than my years.

from the Annals
of John H. Watson, M.D.
1892

". . . plain wooden seats . . ."

Chapter I
The Lady in the Train

Following the successful conclusion of the case known as "The Mark of the Beast," Sherlock Holmes and I parted company in Quebec city. Holmes had business of his own to attend to, and indeed, being officially "deceased," what better opportunity could he have to explore private aspects of his life which the glare of publicity had previously denied him?

For my part, I was pleased to resume some control of my own life, and I resolved to take the opportunity to fulfil a request that had been made of me before leaving London. A senior member at Bart's, under whom I had studied tropical medicine, and with whom I had remained in touch over the years, was concerned for the safety and well-being of his son. The young man, from all accounts, could not be considered wayward, yet like many well-bred youthful Englishmen of the time, down from Cambridge, restless with conditions at home, he had travelled for a year or two in the Colonies, and was now seeking his fortune in Canada, "land of promise." His father had not heard from him since he had left home.

At that particular time, the British Government was offering substantial inducements in the way of land and basic farming equipment to attract prospective settlers to Canada.

I knew little about the boy other than his father's words — " . . . jolly good shot, actually; fond of horses . . ." — which were little enough to go on. The address I had for him was that of an agency in Toronto, Ontario, some five hundred miles west of the city of Quebec, where I now found myself. When one considers that Britain from Land's End to John o' Groats is but 350 miles in its entirety, one gets some sense of the incredible size of this noble country.

The Canadian government was encouraging immigration to fill the vast land to the westward, and had completed a railway to link the country, three thousand miles from the Atlantic Ocean on one side to the Pacific on the other. As fast as the steamships embarked at the ports of Quebec and Montreal, floods of newcomers, both well-to-do and from the labouring classes, arrived, not only from England, Scotland and Ireland, but from many of the countries of Europe, such as the Ukraine and Scandinavia. Some were victims of religious persecution; all were seeking opportunity for themselves in the new land.

It was into a train filled with such immigrants that I bundled myself with the luggage I carried, in the port of Quebec, one bright day in September 1892.

Some of the carriages were laid on for the use of immigrants travelling on a fixed fee, many of whom possessed only the clothes they stood up in. These "coaches" had little more than plain wooden seats to accommodate the passengers. A great wood stove at one end provided warmth and a means whereby travellers could cook their own meals. I had heard of trains stopping in the middle of a field so that passengers could get out and stretch their legs. I heard, too, of a young couple seeking nourishment for an orphan child, who prevailed upon the conductor to stop the train so they could extract milk from a cow that was standing in a field conveniently near the railway track.

For those passengers who could afford it, there were carriages with some amenities, padded seats, gas lights and so on, and it was into one of these that I climbed. I say "climbed" advisedly, because these Canadian trains, built to span a continent, were like giants compared to their English counterparts. There was vast hissing of steam, clouds of black smoke, and a rain of fine cinders from the smokestack. There was a lugubrious clanging of a great bell that the locomotive carried, but why the bell I cannot imagine, since the monster was also equipped with an equally mournful steam-whistle. The interior of my "coach" was reasonably quiet, padded, and panelled. The green velour seats had white lacy antimacassars spread on the headrests.

The carriage was already quite full of travellers, some newly-arrived from Europe, couples and families, their fresh and eager faces bearing a kind of innocence, a shining quality, in marked contrast to those whose pale visages and priestly garments or dark business suits, attaché cases and French-Canadian speech, proclaimed the *ancien régime de Québec.*

For a moment or two I stood in the entrance to the carriage, adjusting my eyes to the interior and looking for a possible seat. I was about to move further down the coach, when I felt a light tap on my arm. I turned, and there beside me in the corner closest to the door, in a double seat otherwise unoccupied, sat a young lady. I would have passed her by had she not reached out and touched me.

"Forgive me, sir" — the voice was English, low and well-modulated — "but do you speak English?"

Eyes the colour of a Highland brook, lips like pink coral. I was aware of her slender hand on my arm, the flow of her modest dove-grey dress, the fashionable hat in the French style.

"Er — yes, I do," I said.

"Then perhaps you can help me."

For all of my reputation with women on three separate continents, I must admit that I am still clumsy when suddenly confronted with female loveliness, particularly beauty in distress.

"Madame?" I queried stiffly.

For a moment her amber eyes met mine. They filled with tears. "I — I'm sorry, sir. Do forgive me."

She withdrew her hand, and turned again to the window. She sought a handkerchief, with which she dabbed her eyes. Beyond the window on the platform, I could see the blurred, hurrying figures of travellers and porters, the carts of luggage, and the usual paraphernalia of an active railway station.

I regretted my bluntness, but I did not know how to redeem myself. She was still turned away.

"Madame," I said, "I have no wish to intrude."

I raised my hat and bowed. I was about to go, but a fresh wave of passengers flowed in, pushing past me with bag and baggage, talking in a language — central-European I suppose — which was quite incomprehensible to me. I rescued my bag from under their feet, and to get out of the way I plumped into the vacant seat facing the lady. She looked up, startled.

"I beg your pardon, madame, the crowd. . . ."

"Oh, yes." She looked quite distraught. "The train is about to leave, sir, is it not?"

I pulled out my pocket watch, snapped it open, and glanced at it. "In a few minutes, if we are on time."

"My — fiancé was to meet me."

"Ah!"

"But he has not arrived."

"He still has time, madame." I gave her my best professional smile, put away my watch, and bent down to retrieve my bag. The lady misinterpreted my move.

"Oh, don't go," she cried.

I glanced around the carriage. It was full.

"There is by now no other vacant seat in the carriage, madame," I said.

I opened my bag and took out a book. I looked up to find the lady watching me. I held up the paper-bound volume.

"I was about to read," I said, "as is my custom while travelling."

She glanced at the book in my hand, reading the title, then smiled suddenly, meeting my eye as if we shared a secret. "*La vie parisienne*," she said.

I found myself blushing slightly, embarrassed. "It passes the time, madame." I opened the book and started to read, but, aware of her presence, I was unable to concentrate. I looked up again to find her gazing at me, a question in her eyes. "Madame?"

"I do not wish to intrude. . . ."

"Not at all, madame."

"Then, may I ask, what is your destination?"

"I am going to Ontario, to look into a purchase of land there, made recently by the son of a friend of mine."

"How curious!" She seemed delighted and clapped her hands.

"How so, madame?"

"My associate and I are doing much the same thing . . . that is, if he has not run into difficulty. . . ." She looked out the window again, close to tears.

I closed my book. "Perhaps I can do something to help, madame."

"That is very kind of you, sir." She turned back to me, eyes glistening. "But I am not sure. . . ."

". . . How useful I might be?" I smiled reassuringly. "Try me, madame."

"Well, then. We made arrangements with Messrs. Blunt and Company of Wardour Street in London — a legitimate land agent, is it not?"

"To the best of my knowledge," I responded.

"They showed us pictures of an Ontario property: a nice farm of some two hundred acres, a house built in the Tudor fashion, outbuildings for livestock. . . ."

"*Tudor* fashion, madame?"

"Yes, quite well set up. Servants' quarters, a small house for the manager. . . ."

"I have not been to Ontario, madame, but it does sound rather grand."

"I am told there is a contract to raise horses for the C.P. Railway. All in all, an attractive proposition, would you not agree, sir?" She smiled at me eagerly.

"Well. . . ." I said.

"So we decided to come over and have a look at it. If it proved not to our liking, we would return to England via New York, having had a nice holiday."

"An expensive holiday, surely!"

"It is a modest sum, all considered, sir. The down payment only."

At this moment, the train shuddered under some heavy impact, and the lady looked up, startled. Outside the carriage window, workmen passed by through escaping steam.

"I think they are coupling on additional carriages," I observed. "We have a few minutes."

"No, I must go," she said. "He — my associate has my bags."

"You still haven't told me your problem, madame."

"It is simple, sir. The agent who is to meet us here, wants his deposit in gold sovereigns. And we have only bank notes." She fumbled in her handbag and produced a tooled Morocco leather wallet, which she opened. "Bank of Canada. There are a hundred dollars here. My associate has a similar sum. Plus a bank draft for emergencies."

"I trust your agent is not a rascal, madame."

"No, I think not. A misunderstanding only, which I'm sure can be remedied. We will straighten it out and catch the next train. Thank, you sir, for your sympathy." She rose and turned to go.

"Madame," said I, "I have gold."

"Sir!" Her dress rustled as she turned to me again, her lovely head held high. "What are you suggesting?"

"Simply, I give you gold for your Bank of Canada notes, and your problem is solved. How much is it you need?"

She fixed me with her clear gaze. "How do you know that I am an honest person?" she demanded.

"Madame, I was not, as they say, born yesterday." I reached into my money belt, and extracted a packet of coin of the realm. "Would ten sovereigns be sufficient?"

She hesitated for a moment, then took the small packet from my hand. "Quite sufficient, sir," she said, "Thank you. I shall leave you with this, in good faith." The lady pressed the wallet into my hand, thrust a visiting card into my breast pocket, and she was gone — a rustle of silk broadcloth and the elusive fragrance of perfume on the smoky air.

I turned the Morocco leather wallet over in my hands. I opened it, and looked at its contents. When I peered out of the carriage window onto the platform, the lady was nowhere in sight. I closed the wallet and put it away safely in an inside pocket.

After a few uneasy minutes, I got up and went to the open door of the carriage. The train bell tolled as if for a funeral, and fine soot from the engine rained down upon me. The lady had vanished. I took her card from my breast pocket. It read *Genevieve la Chance* and gave an address in Chelsea Walk, London. From the card came a faint perfume. The train conductor was waving his flag, a whistle blew, and the train doors were banging shut.

The train began to move. Neither Genevieve la Chance nor her "associate" was to be seen.

". . . built to span a continent . . ."

       (first transcontinental arrives at Port Moody, B.C.)

Chapter II
A Tiger Is Loosed

I had scarcely regained my seat when the door to the next carriage burst open, and a heavy man in his forties entered so precipitately that, as the train picked up speed, he was almost flung into my lap. He carried an expensive leather travelling bag, somewhat worn, which he dropped on the floor of the speeding train in order to arrest his unwilling flight. He recovered his equilibrium, breathing heavily with exertion.

"Sorry!" he said.

His voice had an American twang, and his florid face was wet with perspiration as he slumped into the seat so recently vacated by the lady Genevieve la Chance.

"These gol-darned Canadian trains!" He pulled out a handkerchief and mopped his streaming brow. "Boy, oh, boy!"

This odd utterance seemed to relieve the man's feelings somewhat. He put away his handkerchief and opened his travelling bag, from which he produced a silver flask. He unscrewed the cap and, putting the flask to his lips, he partook deeply of its contents. Then, with every sign of satisfaction, he wiped his mouth with the back of his hand. The man half-rose in his seat, and looked down the length of the carriage. He sat down again and put away his flask.

"Say, buddy." He leaned towards me. "You been sittin'
here long?"

"Ten minutes or so. Why?"

"Did you by any chance see a lady? Young. Grey outfit,
brown eyes, a real good-looker. English accent, no baggage."

"Yes," I replied, "I had that pleasure."

"Pleasure, huh?" He grinned. "So where'd she go?"

"She got off the train."

"Got off the train! I was supposed to meet her here!"
The man was displeased. "Did you talk to her?"

"Yes. Briefly."

"What did ya talk about?"

"She was afraid that her travelling companion — you,
presumably" — my voice was tinged with sarcasm — "had
missed the train. And she did not, apparently, wish to go
without you."

"Oh, boy!" exclaimed my companion, inelegantly. He
thumped the arm rest with his fist. "Women! I'd better find
the porter."

So saying, he got to his feet, and, swaying with the
movement of the speeding train, he set off down the coach,
pushing past the immigrant passengers settling in for the first
stage of their long journey west.

I went back to my book, conscious that I had in my
pocket a hundred dollars in crisp new bank notes which I
had received from the lady, in exchange for but ten pounds
in gold sovereigns.

Somewhere in the Eastern Townships the train pulled into a
siding, with much puffing, hissing of brakes, and clanking of
connecting links. The very size of these Canadian monsters
continues to amaze me, used as I am to the modest 4:01

from Paddington, chuffing through the quiet English countryside. It is a matter of scale, I suppose. These Canadian trains, after all, were designed to carry their loads all the way to the Pacific Ocean. The railway line had recently been cut clear through the Rocky Mountains, bridging awesome chasms and penetrating the stone walls of the mountains.

My surly acquaintance had rejoined me, saying that he had arranged to go as far as Montreal, at which point he would disembark and wait for his "lady friend." The railway telegraph system seemed remarkably efficient in this country, despite the great distances.

I wiped the moisture from the carriage window. It was dark outside, but sporadic light from acetylene lamps showed that additional cars were being added to the train. In the darkness, behind the hissing of steam and the clanking of train links, I thought I heard sounds I had not experienced since my days in India: the roar of a Bengal tiger, mingled with the trumpet of a bull elephant. These exotic sounds came distorted to my ear, submerged as they were under the clanking and hissing of our mechanical monster.

Outside my window, silhouetted against the work lights, a team of workmen came by, tapping the wheels of the train with a hammer. By this means the educated ear could tell if a wheel, perchance, were cracked, and if indeed, the safety of the train were at stake. But by the time they had moved on, all seeming to be well, the links with the additional carriages were accomplished, and with due ceremony, puffing of steam, and grinding of wheels, our train once again got underway. Perhaps the roar of the tiger was for me conjured out of the darkness of the unfamiliar Canadian wilderness.

I had been informed that the train had what was termed a "diner," and presently I set forth in search of it. My companion had opened his bag again, and from it had produced half a cold chicken and a bottle of wine.

I thought again of the hundred dollars in notes that had been pressed upon me by this gross fellow's "lady friend," and I wondered briefly whether to introduce the subject to him, but decided to hold off. I was not totally ignorant of confidence trickery — "con games," as our American cousins would have it.

I pushed through the inter-connecting doors to the next coach, swaying for a moment between the carriages as the mighty wheels thundered over the steel track, scant feet below me.

I gained the relative quiet and modest elegance of the dining car. There was white linen on the tables, and the waiters moved decorously, swaying with the motion of the rushing train. The "silver," as they called it — the knives, forks and spoons — rattled on the immaculate linen.

The car was quite full of French-Canadian businessmen on their way to Montreal, discussing with the waiters in their peculiar *joual* the merits of various wines. They used many gestures and explosive sounds, which I must admit I found theatrical. Yet I envied them. There was such spontaneity, and such a sensual pleasure in their actions, that I felt pallid by comparison.

A waiter approached me.

"M'sieur?" he said.

"Je. . . ." I said, then, "do you speak English?"

"Yes, of course, m'sieur."

"Then," said I, "what do you recommend?"

"We 'ave some fresh cod, sir. An' may I suggest 'alf a bottle of Beaujolais to wash it down?"

"You may indeed," said I. "Capital!"

". . . modest elegance of the dining car . . ."

"M'sieur," he said, and withdrew.

The seat opposite me was vacant. But at that moment the door into the dining car opened. There was a cacophony from the rushing wheels, a shower of steam and cinders. The door closed, and a figure stood there, looking about with bright blue eyes. The fellow was hard to place. He certainly was not a French-Canadian businessman on his way to a meeting in Montreal. Neither indeed was he a moneyed farmer heading for the Prairies. Curiously, he reminded me of figures I had observed in the Punjab, those Hindi fakirs, the snake charmers, those magicians who are said to throw a rope into the air and send a small boy to climb up it, poised there in space. Yet there was nothing in his costume to suggest this, though he was dressed flamboyantly in bright colours, a red riding jacket, a yellow waistcoat, black-and-white checked trousers, all set off by the angle at which he wore a black billycock hat.

He cast a blue eye in my direction, and in a moment had approached the table at which I sat. When he spoke, his voice was a soft Irish brogue. "If this place is not taken, sorr, may I sit here?" He had taken off his billycock, and exposed a shiny bald pate.

"Indeed," said I. "Glad of your company, I'm sure."

The waiter was back, uncorking the half bottle of Beaujolais for my pleasure. He poured a little into my glass and stood back, awaiting my opinion. I sipped the wine.

"Excellent," I said.

"Bon, m'sieur," responded the waiter, and he filled my glass.

The fish arrived, hot off the grill. It was accompanied by fried potatoes, "french fried" as they are termed here. I tucked in, realising how hungry I was.

"M'sieur?" The waiter regarded my table companion.

"I'll have the fish and chips, and a bottle of beer."

"We only 'ave the wine, m'sieur."

"Wine, then. That's fine with me."

Along with his unusual get-up, I realized that my companion had an air of quiet authority. His voice had *timbre*, as the French say. He sat there quite relaxed, looking over the formal French businessmen, and after a moment he spoke.

"You are not one of them."

"Sir?"

"You're not French."

"Oh, no, no, indeed."

"English?"

"Yes."

"Newly arrived, I should say."

"Yes, you might say that."

"On business?"

"Private business." I sipped my wine and looked at him. "Why do you ask?"

"Just my everlasting curiosity, sir." He grinned amicably and passed his hand over his naked scalp. "In this country we get in the habit of asking questions, getting acquainted. . . . Such a big land, and so few people. It is sometimes interpreted by newcomers as rudeness."

"Ah," I said. I got on with my fish, not wishing to encourage him. When the waiter arrived with the fellow's dinner, I noticed they didn't go through the wine-tasting formality. The waiter simply put down the food, uncorked the bottle of wine, and departed.

"There you go, eh?" said my companion. "It's all in the appearance. Old World class distinction. Even over here."

"I suppose so," I said.

The fellow ate and drank with some relish. After a few minutes, he looked up.

"Did you notice, a little while ago, the train stopped to attach some extra cars?" he asked, his blue eyes glinting at me.

"I did," I responded.

"Did you notice anything unusual?" he asked. He dabbed at his mouth with his table napkin.

"Since you mention it," I said, "I could have sworn I heard the roar of a Bengal tiger."

"Right you are, sir," said my companion with a note of pleasure. "A Bengal tiger! Here in the wilds of Canada! Very observant of you, sir!" He grinned at me approvingly and went on with his food.

"You have some connection with this animal?" I asked.

"Yes indeed, sir," he replied. "If I may introduce myself . . . I am . . . the Fabulous Flaherty, of Flaherty's Travelling Circus! Jack, to my friends. At your service, sir."

"Oh," said I.

"And you, sir?"

"Watson. John Watson, M.D."

"The pleasure is mine, Doctor Watson," said my new acquaintance, and he tucked into his food with renewed vigour.

The light gleamed upon his bald pate, and his fringe of white hair quivered as he ate. After a moment or two he looked up again with his sharp blue eye.

"India, eh?" he said.

"Punjab," I replied. "Afghan Wars."

"Ah! Learned to use a gun, did you?"

"I was a medical officer."

"Pistols, perhaps."

"Yes, I have used a pistol," I said carefully, wondering what he was getting at.

"Do you have one with you?"

"Yes, in fact, I do. In my luggage . . . why would you ask a question like that, sir?"

"Well, in confidence," he leaned towards me, and lowered his voice, "I'm a bit concerned about my tiger."

"Oh. Tiger."

"Been off his feed — moody-like. You can never tell with tigers of a certain age."

"No, I suppose you can't."

"Don't like travelling cooped up."

So saying, he sat back again, and refreshed himself with his glass of wine, the matter apparently dismissed. The waiter had arrived with coffee and some sort of dessert pudding. I waved the latter away, and I must say that I had tasted better coffee. In any event, with the help of a cigar, I quieted the inner man. The waiter had left a modest enough bill for the meal, and reaching into my pocket to pay for it, my hand encountered the leather wallet that the lady Genevieve la Chance had virtually thrust upon me. Without thought, I pulled it out and opened it.

I was conscious of the alert eyes of my table companion, as he leaned towards me again and spoke in a low voice.

"That's rather a lot of money to be flashing about, sir, if I may say so."

I extracted a five dollar note from the wallet, and restored the latter to my pocket.

"Yes, thank you. That was inadvertent. . . ."

I was eager to get back to my privacy, my book, and my own thoughts, away from the company of chance-met strangers. I called the waiter and gave him the five dollars. He gave me change in return. I paid for my modest meal, tipped the fellow, nodded to my table companion, and made my way back to my carriage.

Upon gaining my seat, I found my American fellow traveller sprawled in a corner, eyes closed, his head wobbling with the passage of the train. In his lap were the remains of his chicken. He was occupying more than half of the seat, and as I stood there for a moment, annoyed, the motion of the train rolled an empty wine bottle from under the seat. It bumped my foot, and I picked it up, uncertain as to my next move.

It was not long in coming. There was a sudden, sustained rush of sound as our train passed another, heading in the opposite direction. The air pressure between the two monsters was tangible, and the carriage in which I stood swayed under its impact. Then, before my eyes, yielding to gravitational forces of the rushing train, the unconscious figure before me slid slowly to the floor, limp as a rag doll.

I kneeled down beside the inert figure and felt for his pulse. There was none.

I have faced sudden death many times in my life, both in war and in peace. In a way it is part of my stock in trade, and yet to meet it unexpectedly on the floor of this behemoth of a train, rushing through the night of an unknown land, made my scalp prickle.

The door at the far end of the carriage opened with a blast of sound and cold air. I looked up, half-expecting to see the reassuring figure of my dear friend Holmes, arriving to take charge, but of course it was not he. Coming down the crowded aisle towards me was the head steward of the dining car. In his hand he clutched the five dollar note I had given him. I had no doubt that he was looking for me, so I stood up and waited for him. He saw me and approached.

"Pardon, m'sieur, mais. . . ."

His glance shifted as he discovered the crumpled form on the floor. He looked at me again, then at the bottle in my hand. "Quoi? Est-il inébriant?"

"Non. Il est mort."

"Mort?"

"Yes," I said. "Quite mort."

The steward looked down the carriage at the sleeping forms of my fellow passengers. No-one paid us any attention. He turned back to me.

"Mais. . . ." He looked from me to the body, to the note still clutched in his hand.

"Is there a problem about that?" I asked.

"This, m'sieur?" He held up the money as if he had just discovered it.

"Yes. It is good, is it not?"

"Ah, oui, m'sieur, of the best . . ." His eyes strayed to the body.

"Well, then?"

"It is just that the number on it corresponds to a list we 'ave of money stolen." He looked up at me again.

"Stolen?"

"Yes, m'sieur. A bank robbery in Ottawa, two days ago. . . . In such an affair we 'ave a list in the railway of numbers, also our h'instructions."

"Well then, I shall replace it." I reached into my pocket.

"But, m'sieur, I should. . . ."

I produced two five dollar bills from my own wallet, and waved them under his nose. "These are reputable bills of the Bank of Nova Scotia," I said, and slipped them into his breast pocket.

"Ah, m'sieur!" murmured the poor fellow dubiously.

I moved to take the crisp new Bank of Canada note from between his fingers. But he pulled his hand away, the note still in it, uncertainty written on his honest face.

At this moment the door opened at the far end of the carriage, and Jack Flaherty the circus man entered. He made his way towards us, and nodded in recognition as he squeezed past. He glanced at the figure collapsed on the floor, at the empty wine bottle in my hand, and smiled at me sympathetically. There was a rush of air as he opened the connecting door, then he was gone.

"Another friend of yours, m'sieur?"

"Neither is a friend of mine, waiter."

"This one 'ere,'" he gestured to the body on the floor. "You are sure 'e is, er — mort?"

"I am a doctor," I replied stiffly.

"Bien, a docteur," he shrugged. "Well, docteur, what am I to do? First, wit' every respect, docteur, you give me money which proves to be stolen. Then, this gentilhomme wit' whom you appear to be travelling, is dead!"

"I am not travelling with him!" I retorted.

"Bien, it is a matter beyond my comprehension, m'sieur." He peered at the recumbent figure on the floor, desiring, I think, to raise it like Lazarus from the grave. That failing, he looked around the carriage as if for inspiration, then after a moment, his mind made up, turned towards me again.

"Bien, m'sieur, I must seek authority. What best to do . . . and, m'sieur, perhaps it is best" — from his breast pocket he took the two Bank of Nova Scotia notes that I had thrust upon him, and pressed them into my hand — "it is best that you keep this money, and I shall keep this" — he held up the confounded Bank of Canada note — "until we find out what is what. And if you will excuse me, m'sieur, I must take the responsibility invested in me by the railroad to tell you, you must remain 'ere until this matter is investigated."

He stood erect, bowed to me formally, and turning, he set off away from me down the length of the sleeping coach. I could not help but admire the manner in which the steward had handled the affair, treading the narrow line between responsibility to his employer and his own self-interest.

As for myself, it was not the first time that I had had an unexpected corpse on my hands, although usually if it was anything out of the ordinary, my good friend Sherlock Holmes would be there to advise me.

Empty wine bottle still in hand, I stepped over the recumbent body of the stranger and sat down to await events. As I made myself tolerably comfortable, it occurred to me that anyone aware of the circumstances would think we had, like other occupants of the carriage, simply settled down for the night, aided perhaps by the ingestion of a shared bottle of wine.

The wine. A few dregs still remained in the bottle. As a qualified physician, I had quickly determined that the fellow was quite dead. The cause of his death was another matter. I sniffed cautiously at the bottle. A modest French red, of no particular merit. There was no foreign odour as of poison — at least not to my nose. Perhaps laboratory analysis would reveal something more, but that was up to the authorities, not to me. I put down the bottle on the seat opposite, beside the man's Gladstone bag. I noticed that the bag was unfastened, gaping by an inch or two, and for a moment or two I thought to search it, to gain perhaps some information about the stranger. In the end, however, I simply reached over and snapped it shut.

I tried to go back to my book, but I was increasingly troubled by the realization of my own situation. I could see myself trying to explain to the French-Canadian police how it was I had a hundred dollars of stolen money in my pocket, and a corpse under my feet. An American corpse, furthermore. Confound the fair sex! For I felt that my courtesy to the lady Genevieve was responsible for my predicament. My fingers reached into my breast pocket for the calling card she had given me. I took it out and looked at it for a moment. Its faint scent was a momentary echo of her — I must admit — delightful, tantalizing presence. I turned it over, half-expecting to find a cryptic message or an address on the back, giving me a clue to her whereabouts, but there was nothing to be seen.

I had no sooner restored the visiting card to my breast pocket than the interconnecting door again opened, and Flaherty reappeared, and came directly to me, his voice low but businesslike.

"If you have your revolver, sir. Perhaps you could assist."

"What?" I asked stupidly, looking up at him.

"The tiger, sir."

"Good Lord!" I responded. I opened my bag and groped in it for my weapon and half-a-dozen cartridges. I followed the man.

Upon gaining the back of the train, an extraordinary sight greeted me. Flaherty's Travelling Circus seemingly was able to "travel" simply by owning two railway cars. One contained the animals and properties for their performance, the other the performers and animal trainers and their living arrangements; the cars could be dropped off on a railroad siding adjacent to any town or settlement big enough to provide a paying audience.

What greeted my eyes was bizarre in the extreme. Although I was not entirely unfamiliar with the Big Top in various parts of the world, as an occasional paying member of the audience, this was the first time that I had been privileged to be behind the scenes in the diverse, self-sufficient world of the circus.

At first I saw no sign of the voracious tiger that had been announced. There were a few enclosures and cages containing exotic beasts — an Indian elephant, a camel and a buffalo from the Western plains — and a few horses. The animals seemed peaceful enough, either asleep or munching on hay. What caught my eye was the human activity which filled the rest of the limited space. The circus folk contrived, within the confines of the railway carriage, to cook and eat, to exercise, and to practise their demanding circus routines and stunts.

As I entered, I was confronted by a giant of a man dressed in a moth-eaten leopard skin, who occupied himself with lifting three spangled ladies in the air; poised between his horny hands and his immense lion's mane of a head, they occupied themselves with twirling a bewildering array of coloured hoops. There was not enough headroom in the carriage for such activity, so the giant knelt down, the better to accommodate the activity of his pretty consorts.

In front of an elephant stall, mixing some kind of mash in a wooden trough, a dark-complexioned man no more than three feet high turned his eyes on me and smiled, his lips crinkling back and exposing teeth filed to points and red with some stuff he was chewing. On his shoulder was a monkey, who chattered at me, then leaped onto a bunch of bananas which hung from the coach roof. The pygmy turned to the elephant and grunted in a curious manner, to which the creature responded with high-flung trunk and a trumpet of pleasure. At least I supposed it to be pleasure, since he was about to be fed.

I became aware of another sound, a pulsating feline snarl, which made my nerve ends quiver. I had not heard its like since my days in Bengal — the challenge of an angry tiger. It came again, this time a high-pitched scream, a sound which cut through the rumble of the train and the incidental protests of the lesser animals in the car. The horrific sound seemed to come from the other end of the carriage, beyond the other animals and their escorts.

I was then aware that I had not yet loaded my revolver, and as I turned my attention to it in the crowded space, Flaherty's pink face reappeared, shining with sweat under its bowler hat. He caught my eye, looking worried, and I held up a bullet to reassure him. The tiger was quiet for a moment, and I started to load. Flaherty glanced away from me nervously as the elephant moved uneasily in his stall. I clicked my Webley shut, and was ready to proceed, but at that moment the tiger screamed again, sounding more angry than before, the voice of the beast vibrating in the enclosed space of the rushing railway carriage. My hair virtually stood on end, and I felt an astonishing atavistic response that touched the very fibres of my being. I braced myself to move and confront the creature. But at this moment another curious sound came to my ears. It was a melodious four-note pattern of music, played on some kind of pipe. Two or three times the phrase was repeated. The tiger roared again, but at less volume than before. The pipe continued over and over, repeating its hypnotic phrase, up and down, now seeming to fill the carriage with its sound, now fading to a whisper. The tiger's protests were reduced to a rumble.

Flaherty's bowler-hatted head bobbed up again out of the throng. His blue eye caught mine, and he held a blunt forefinger to his lips. He glanced away, then back, then beckoned me gently forward. Activity within the speeding railway car had ceased. The strong man and his girls stood relaxed as if posing for a modern French painting. The little Andaman Islander, for so I supposed him to be, sat grinning to himself, playing with the monkey, who, still perched on his shoulder, was eating a banana. The animals were quiet.

The pipe continued its seductive rise and fall, and under it now, to my astonishment, came a deep baritone, the thrilling sound of a Bengal tiger purring like a great kitten.

Confronting me, at the far end of the carriage, was an empty cage. Its door was open, and from it two attendants were dragging the semiconscious form of a young man. A third attendant was in the cage sluicing away signs of blood, and beside the cage, on the floor, a man sat cross-legged. He wore some kind of Eastern garb, and on his head was a tarbush of dirty felt. At his mouth was a bulbous wind instrument into which he blew, creating the mesmeric melody that continued to suffuse the entire railroad carriage.

Eyes closed, brown fingers moving rhythmically over the pipe, he blew, seemingly oblivious to his background. Most remarkable of all, at the man's feet, fully eight feet from nose to tail, lay a handsome Bengal tiger. Eyes closed, its regal head cradled in the man's lap, for all the world like a great domesticated cat in some woman's kitchen, it lay there, eyes squeezed shut in seeming ecstasy, throat vibrating with a rhythmic purr.

Poised with my revolver, conscious of my own rapid heartbeat, I felt foolish. I looked round for Flaherty, who from under his bowler hat looked back at me, apologetically grinning and lifting his shoulders in a gesture of wonder. The attendants had now distributed some straw and placed some food in the tiger's cage, and in a moment the great beast got up of its own volition, and, still purring, quietly entered the cage, where it commenced to groom itself.

The cage door closed gently on the animal. The man with the pipe ceased to blow his curious hypnotic melody, and the group of circus people got on with their lives as if nothing untoward had occurred.

"I'm sorry to have called ye in here, sir," said Flaherty. "It looked like an emergency for a bit."

"Your man seemed to have it well in hand," I replied, unloading my revolver. My voice trembled a little, much to my annoyance. "For which I am very grateful."

I put the loose shells in my pocket and turned to the fellow in the tarbush.

"Good Lord!" I exclaimed.

"Hello, Watson," said Sherlock Holmes.

Chapter III
I Am Imprisoned and Escape

Kingston, Ontario, is largely built of local white granite, which sparkles in the summer sun. Construction of the Rideau Canal, conceived during the War of 1812 to provide a safe waterway between Montreal and Upper Canada, gave impetus to the growth of the town, and at the time of my visit it had a population of fifteen thousand. From its active port ply steamships and sailing vessels, carrying passengers and trade far into the interior of the country, and to the United States. From its military base, Fort Henry, in the east end of the community, issue the commands and responses of young, élite Canadian army officers in training. At the other end of town, a darker structure squats beside the lake. Stone turrets mark the corners of its high granite walls, and in the turrets, armed guards are posted. It is Kingston Penitentiary.

"There is such a thing as making a prison too comfortable, and the prisoner too happy," Canada's Prime Minister John A. Macdonald is quoted in the year 1871. I suppose Sir John should know. After all, he practised law in Kingston before he became prime minister, and he was buried in Kingston after his death in 1891, shortly before my own visit to the aforementioned Kingston Penitentiary.

From my experience there, I would have liked to reassure Sir John that indeed, for the inmates of Kingston, life was not a happy one. I suppose the difference is one of viewpoint. If you visit the gaol on a conducted tour, as a political figure of some prominence, you perhaps see one thing. If you are incarcerated there for a misdemeanour, you see quite another.

Envisage, if you will, within those massive walls, a barred cell, not one inch wider than the bed, and which in length has only a couple of feet to spare. This is where I would myself be confined after a series of unfortunate occurrences which arose from innocent well-meaning actions on my part, in the service, as I thought, of my fellow human-beings.

First, there was the incident involving the charming lady, Genevieve la Chance, with whom my misadventures began, for it was due to my kindness to her that I was carrying one hundred crisp new notes in stolen money, which the police had found upon me. Madame la Chance had vanished and left me to face her music. What had not vanished was the body of her American friend, who could have cleared up the matter, I am sure, had he been able.

When the train arrived in Montreal, the police had carted away the body for investigation, and had clapped me under arrest. I had anticipated some intervention from my friend Holmes, but there was no further sign of him. While I was tied up with the Montreal authorities, the circus vans had been uncoupled from the train and had vanished as if they were a figment of my imagination — circus, animals, the cocky blue-eyed figure of Flaherty, the dark-skinned betel-nut-chewing Andaman native with his pointed teeth, and, of course, my one good friend in the world, Sherlock Holmes himself.

After police interrogation in Montreal, I had been brought to Kingston and held in the penitentiary pending further investigation. At once, of course, I had retained legal counsel, counsel, in fact, from the very office of the eminent lawyer Sir John A., the recently deceased Prime Minister of Canada, who had done so much for his country. I only hoped that his legal inheritors could do half as well for me.

There was a rattle at my cell door. A key was inserted in the ponderous lock. The heavy barred door swung open. It was one of the guards.

"Visitor to see you. Follow me."

I followed him along the echoing range. The prison, I suppose, was quite advanced for its time. Charles Dickens seemed to like it when he visited the place a few years earlier, even though he seems to have been more interested in the female inmates than in the prison itself.

Certainly, Dickens seemed not to have heard of the incarceration a few years earlier of eight-year-old children, who were repeatedly subjected to the lash because they did not maintain silence. Or the French-Canadian child, who suffered a similar fate for speaking French in this English-speaking establishment!

Ponderous barred doors opened up for us, and closed firmly behind us, their clang echoing from the stone walls. We went down steel steps and across the granite floor of the "Dome" — the high arching centre of the building, from which tiered ranges of cells radiated evilly, like the web of a monstrous spider. Presently I found myself within the stone walls of a small room, illuminated by a single barred window.

Waiting for me was my lawyer, a thin, bird-like young fellow in his mid-thirties, a certain quizzical authority in his eye, nervous energy in his movements. "Doctor Watson?" He looked at me sharply. "It *is* Doctor, is it not, sir?"

"It is indeed," said I.

"Well then," said he, placing his top hat on a worn briefcase on the table between us, "please sit down."

We both did so, and he opened his briefcase. "I have followed up the references you have given me, sir." He produced a pair of pince-nez, clipped them on the bridge of his nose, and through them peered at his documents. "And I must say, I am more than a little puzzled."

"Puzzled?" I asked.

"First, you give me the name of a lady, chance-met on a train between Quebec and Montreal."

"In Quebec," I corrected, "in the railway station. In the train. Before the train departed, she got off and I did not see her again."

My young lawyer looked at me over his pince-nez. "She gave you, you say, one hundred dollars in Bank of Canada notes — a not inconsiderable sum of money — in exchange for ten golden sovereigns."

"Yes, that is correct."

"Why?"

"I thought I had explained all that."

"A lady in distress."

"Yes."

"To the tune of ten sovereigns?"

"Yes," said I, feeling a fool. Was I to tell him that I was bowled over by the woman?

He peered at me again over his confounded pince-nez. "I am informed that the notes were, in fact, part of the proceeds of a bank robbery which had occurred in Ottawa the previous day."

"So I am now given to understand."

"My information is that the lady in question is a person of unblemished character and reputation."

"Of that I have no doubt," said I gallantly.

"And yet you insist that the sum of one hundred dollars Canadian currency, found in your possession and identified as money stolen from the Bank of Canada, came to you from this same lady."

"I do."

He gazed at me for a moment, then took a handkerchief, and blew his nose. "Indeed," he said.

He tucked his hanky up his sleeve, a habit I have always deplored, and turned again to his portfolio. "Let us turn our attention to the dead man . . . the deceased . . . an American, I am given to understand. You stated that when you returned from the dining car and found this individual 'asleep,' as you thought him to be, your foot struck an empty wine bottle on the floor of the railway carriage beneath him. You stooped and picked it up, and you had it in your hand when the head steward of the dining car approached you. It is all recorded here." He gestured to the pages in his brief.

"Yes." I continued to be patient.

"There were dregs of wine in the bottle."

"I believe so."

"Well, I must tell you that the dregs of wine were subsequently analysed, and found to contain a poisonous substance!"

It was not the first time that this sort of thing had passed my way, and I was not unduly impressed.

"What kind of poison?" I asked.

"Ergot," said the lawyer, looking at his papers. "Some sort of fungus, I am led to believe. As a doctor, you would know of it."

"I know of it. It is hardly lethal."

"The evidence seems to demonstrate otherwise." He looked at his papers again. "When questioned by the police in Montreal," he went on, "you finally gave as a personal character reference the name of one Mr. Sherlock Holmes of London, England."

"Yes, I did," I replied, annoyed in retrospect at my own stupidity.

"I am told that the Montreal Police have been in contact with Scotland Yard in the matter, and they have been informed that Mr. Holmes died in Switzerland, four months ago. He fell over the" — the lawyer checked his notes again — "the Reichenbach Falls, and his body was not recovered. They also say that you, Doctor Watson, were reported to be with Mr. Holmes at the time."

"I cannot deny it," I said.

My legal advisor looked at me sadly. "I must say, sir," he said, "that I do have difficulty in presenting your case in a favourable light. Indeed, I must say that I fail to see that you have any case at all."

"Then what am I to do?" I exclaimed.

"In the absence of a substantial character reference, I am for the moment at a loss to advise you, sir. It is a most unfortunate circumstance. I must wish you good day, sir!"

So saying, my lawyer collected his papers, clapped his top hat on his head, picked up his briefcase, and departed. The guard escorted me back to my cell, and the heavy ironbound door slammed again behind me.

The tiered cells in Kingston Penitentiary radiate from a central point like the web of a spider, as I have observed. Each cell is locked and barred, each tier is locked and barred, and the main gates are locked and barred.

At some hour before dawn, I awakened in my cell, some vagrant ray of moonlight finding its way through the network of bars and steel, probing my consciousness. I had a curious awareness. There had been a low hissing sound, or perhaps a rattling, not of chains or bars, but . . . I had in mind a snake. In this country they have what they called "rattlers" — snakes which reach a length of four or five feet. They are the only deadly snakes to be found in Canadian woods and swamps.

Mindful of the guards and of their arbitrary authority in such places as Kingston Penitentiary, I opened my eyes warily. Far off, a steel door clanged shut. Closer, there was snoring and muttered imprecations, blurred in the sleep of some restless inmate.

It came again, the rattle, very close, and through half-closed eyes I saw in the moon's rays what appeared to be a pair of slim dark hands detached from a human body, which busied themselves for a few moments at the lock to my cell. Then, soundlessly, the door swung open, one of the hands beckoned me, and in a moment, crouched down, curbing my beating heart, I moved towards it.

My cell was on the top tier of the prison. It gave onto a gallery of steel girders — a metal catwalk. Below me, two other levels of cells, behind their barred doors, led as I have described to the ground floor, where I had earlier met my "lawyer."

Above me, the roof curved to the apex of the building, the "Dome," in which were set windows far beyond the reach of any but stray sparrows who found themselves trapped by mischance in this odious place. These windows were designed to provide a modicum of light and ventilation, and so distant were they from the floor of the prison, or indeed from the nearest gallery of cells, that the authorities had not seen fit to equip them with the bars which graced every other opening in the building.

As I crept from my cell, a shadow among shadows arose from the gallery floor. I felt the rough texture of manila rope pass around my body, heard the curious rattling sound again; the rope tightened and I found myself suddenly in flight, rapidly traversing the space between the uppermost tier of cells and the top of the Dome. My rescuer, a veritable monkey, was swarming up the rope ahead of me, hand over hand, like a creature of the jungle. So swiftly did he move that he was already at a window in the Dome by the time I had reached that point. He turned to assist me, and it was then I recognized the grinning face and the red-stained pointed teeth of the little Andaman Islander from Flaherty's Circus.

Rope and all, I squeezed through the opening into the cool night air. From this vantage point one could see, over the granite walls, the sleeping town of Kingston on one hand, on the other the dark water of Lake Ontario, glistening in the moonlight. I had but a moment to make these observations, before my escort joined me, and grasping the rope short to my waist, braced himself against the angle of the window embrasure and pointed down, grinning at me. His meaning was unmistakeable. I was to go over the edge of the roof! I looked down, appalled. My foot slipped, and had it not been for the rope around my waist, I assuredly would have fallen. The native glared at me now, making a frightful visage, ready, I think, to push me off should I prove obstinate. So I took a deep breath and stepped off the narrow window ledge, slithering down the curved surface of the dome, as the fellow took my weight on the rope.

As I descended, I was conscious of a movement in one of the sentry posts on a corner of the high granite walls that enclosed the frightful place. I had been informed that the sentries were equipped with the same efficient Lee-Enfield .303 rifles, stamped *V.R.* for Victoria Regina, that had wrought such havoc on the Afghanistan frontier, and the thought occurred to me how absurd it would be to end my days being used for target practice on the dim moonlit roof of Kingston Penitentiary half a world away.

My feet touched a ledge. A hand touched mine.

"Come along, Watson," said Sherlock Holmes.

Chapter IV
A Matter of Murder

I found myself in a small rowing boat on the moonlit water of Lake Ontario, together with the gibbering aborigine and my good friend Sherlock Holmes. Into my hands Holmes had thrust a fishing line, which now streamed over the stern of the boat into the water. He was rowing gently, and the current took us slowly past the forbidding walls of Kingston Penitentiary, which I had so recently and precipitately vacated.

Every moment I expected an alarm from within the grim walls of the prison, and a fusillade of shots from the Lee-Enfield .303 I had seen cradled in the arms of the prison guard. But no. In fact, a sudden tug on my line signalled that I had caught a fish.

"Good Lord, Holmes! I've caught a jolly fish!"

"Then pull it in, dear chap," came Holmes's reassuring voice.

I did so, and there was a nice fat bass, all of ten inches in length.

"Now bait your hook again, and throw it back in," said Holmes. "There is a can of worms in the bottom of the boat."

I did as I was told, and the dark walls of the prison glided by without further incident.

"Good morning, sir. Your bath is ready."

"What?" I opened my eyes blearily.

"A pot of hot tea, and today's newspaper. Breakfast is in half an hour."

"Oh?" I propped myself on my elbow.

"Your clothes have been cleaned and pressed, sir. Your linen washed and ironed. I trust that everything is satisfactory."

The valet left the room. After a moment, I swung my legs out of bed and looked about me. I was in a well-appointed hotel room. My two travelling bags sat on the floor beside the ornate dresser. I got up and retrieved one of them. I undid the straps, and snapped open the locks. Inside, I discovered my personal belongings intact: money belt, gold sovereigns and all.

I took out my dressing gown and put it on. I poured a cup of tea, an excellent Darjeeling, hot and fragrant. The day brightened. I raised the cup to my lips, and my eye fell on the newspaper headline, "Railway Murder Mystery Deepens." I sipped a little of the tea, and took up the paper.

More evidence has come to light, in the matter of the railway murder of last week. The Coroner's Office revealed this morning that further examination of the corpse disclosed two tiny red marks on the neck, spaced roughly an inch apart. Today, this newspaper has been informed, a small package delivered to the coroner's office proved to contain the body of a brown spider of unknown species. Upon closer examination of the creature, the spacing of its mandibles proved to match the red marks on the neck of the corpse. The dead spider was discovered in the baggage of the deceased during a routine police examination, and forwarded by the Police Department to the Coroner's Office. It is judged by the Coroner's Office that if the spider is of a virulent species, its bite alone could prove fatal. The simultaneous ingestion of a bottle of wine infected with fungus would make doubly sure of its victim, in the opinion of Dr. Jane, the City Coroner.

Ironically, Doctor John H. Watson of London, England, the last man to see the victim alive, lodged at Kingston Penitentiary while the case was being investigated, proved to be no longer in his cell when called upon by the Warden's Office to discharge him.

"He seems to have vanished into thin air," said an embarrassed George Bromby, local resident and prison guard detailed to attend Watson.

A later dispatch on this unusual affair discloses that Mr. G. H. Harrison, lawyer from the offices of the late Sir John A. Macdonald here in Kingston, states that Doctor Watson is none other than the friend and confidant of the late Mr. Sherlock Holmes, universally praised private detective, also of London, England. Doctor Watson's present whereabouts are unknown at the present time, but he has been cleared officially of this grotesque crime. There are at present no further leads in the case.

Upon reading the foregoing, I felt a burden lift from my shoulders, and the cup of Darjeeling tasted even better. I found myself singing in the bathtub, and presently, newly-dressed, I went down to the dining room.

Sherlock Holmes looked up from the menu. "Sleep well?" he asked cheerfully. He looked more or less his old self in a worn tweed jacket and a tie. "Ready for breakfast?"

"Good morning, Holmes," I said. "Yes. Very well. Thank you." I sat down and unfolded my napkin.

"There is porridge with fresh cream, haddock, kidney, bacon and eggs, lamb chops, toast, Scottish marmalade. What is your fancy?"

I looked at him in wonder. "Really, Holmes. . . ."

"What is it, dear chap?"

My mind swirled in response. Having so narrowly avoided what seemed to me a violent miscarriage of justice, having been placed under arrest, summarily tried and clapped in gaol, having in fact being treated as a criminal in this land of the free in a kind response to a cry for help, I knew not what to say. I took a deep breath.

Then I tucked my table napkin firmly under my chin. "Well," I said. "I think . . . I shall start with the porridge, and work my way through the lot!"

"Capital!" cried Holmes. "Waitress, if you please!"

"Holmes, I must thank you for your timely interference on my behalf with the blind wheels of justice," I said presently, my mouth full of kidney and bacon.

"You mean getting you out of Kingston Penitentiary?"

"Quite."

My companion groped in his pocket for a pipe and a packet of the *habitant* tobacco he had grown used to.

"Dear chap, official enquiries as to what actually occurred at the Reichenbach Falls were proving rather embarrassing to Scotland Yard, and indirectly to certain departments of Her Majesty's Government. I am, after all, supposed to be dead, and your using my name as a reference was not, may I say, well-timed."

"Sorry," I said. "Pass the marmalade, would you?"

He pushed the marmalade in my direction. I spread it on another slice of hot, buttered toast.

"Indeed," said Holmes, lighting his pipe, "I am requested by my friend Hargreaves, of the New York Police Department, to look into certain matters which touch on American, British and Canadian relations, and to do this, I must retain my incognito status." He gave me a quizzical look.

"Well, good luck with it, Holmes old chap!" said I, now well fortified with a good breakfast. I pulled the copy of the Kingston *Whig Standard* out of my pocket. "It says here in the paper that I am now officially cleared in the matter of the railway murder."

"Quite," said Holmes, exhaling a fragrant cloud of tobacco smoke.

"Which means that, with any luck, I can pick up the threads and get on with my own life again."

"Exactly."

"What do you mean, Holmes, 'exactly'?" I looked at him suspiciously.

He drew on his pipe. "As I understand it, Watson, your intention in staying on in Canada for a bit, is to discover the whereabouts and the circumstances of a young friend of yours. . . ."

" . . . The son of a friend of mine actually, Holmes. . . ."

"Quite," said Holmes. "A young chap of a good English family, down from Cambridge, has done the usual thing, travelled the world, seen the Empire, Africa, India. Now in Canada with a view to settling down, perhaps acquiring a few hundred acres of land, and a staff to run the estate while he rides off to hounds."

"Something like that," I said, nettled.

"His family in England have not heard from him, and they would appreciate your reassurance, since you are here, Watson, as it were, on the spot."

"That is more or less correct, Holmes."

I don't know whether Holmes is aware of his ability, at a stroke, to deflate one's ego. It happens from time to time, and I have come to accept it as a matter of course, although I do not enjoy it.

He blew a cloud of smoke. "Actually," he said, "his father took me into his confidence before we left England. Sought my opinion, in fact."

"Oh, did he? I was under the impression it was a private matter." I sounded aggrieved, and Holmes turned and looked at me.

"Sorry, Watson," he said. "I did not mean to intrude."

"That's all right," I said, and I opened the newspaper with more vigor than strictly necessary.

"Might I enquire, then, what is your next move?" said Holmes, after a moment.

"You may," I replied. "I see advertised here a maritime service between Kingston and Toronto, and I propose to take advantage of it. The steamship *Daffodil* is leaving Kingston this afternoon at three o'clock, and arrives in Toronto sometime tomorrow morning. I intend to be on it."

"Jolly good," said Sherlock Holmes.

Chapter V
Genevieve la Chance

The S.S. *Daffodil* turned out to be a trim little vessel, designed in Glasgow, and built in the busy and not inextensive shipyards in Kingston. The need for shipping on the Great Lakes was considerable, servicing as it did both sides of the border, Canada to the north and America to the south.

The official border between the two great countries runs in an irregular line up the centre of the St. Lawrence River, and more or less down the centre of the Great Lakes. At converging points between the Lakes, as at Niagara, where the magnificent, world-famous falls drop tumultuously over the escarpment, the distance between the two countries is spanned by a footbridge, over which one can cross without hindrance, having at the same time an excellent view of this famous natural phenomenon.

The overnight passage to Toronto passed without incident. I don't know quite what I expected, but the events of the past few days had quite unsettled me, and had I been awakened in the dead of night by the grinning betel-nut-stained visage of the Andaman Islander peering through my porthole, or the chilling sound of a cell door slamming shut upon me, I should not have been surprised.

As it was, I had a quite reasonable dinner on board, and I was fortunate enough to get a tiny but immaculate overnight cabin and a comfortable berth. I slept the sleep of the just, and awakened refreshed, feeling that at last I was on my own, without encumbrance or duty to anyone. I rose, shaved and dressed, and went out on deck.

Understand how delightful and refreshing to me was this scene. Used as I was to the crowded streets of London, dear to me though they were, the shining crystalline surface of the lake in the early morning, the scent of pine trees from the nearby shore, the cry of seagulls as they swooped over us, each was a source of pleasure to me beyond my ability to express. In this happy state of mind, I went down to breakfast.

The map of Toronto lay like a grid on the landscape. Unlike the centuries-old cities I was acquainted with, built on the estuaries of rivers, or radiating from fortress-like centres, Toronto, newly-born, seemed bound only by the gleaming waters of Lake Ontario to the south, and to the north by primeval wilderness. Within those limits, her exuberant growth knew no bounds. Her main streets, I was told, had grown up along Indian trails used for centuries as portage routes from one body of water to another, for hunting and fur-trading, and I suppose, for bloodthirsty intertribal warfare. Yonge Street, which extended from the busy docks of the waterfront, up through the centre of the city, had been such a portage route. It now served those who, acquiring large tracts of property, were turning the primeval forests into lush farmland. Beyond that, the road continued to the waterways of the Georgian Bay, from whence, traditionally, voyageurs and fur-traders could take their birch-bark canoes north and west, another thousand miles into the wilderness.

". . . gleaming waters of Lake Ontario . . ."

I registered in the modest York Hotel at the foot of Simcoe Street, adjacent to the docks, and I sought the address I had for the young Honourable Reggie Braithwaite. A not-uncomfortable horse-drawn tramcar drew me through the busy thoroughfares of the town northwards to Bloor Street, another singular avenue which extended for many miles. Near Bloor Street I discovered a row of nicely-built though modest houses, reflecting the excellent work of Scottish masons. Maple trees shadowed the walks. Housewives and servants strolled in leisurely fashion, on their way to shop for daily needs of kitchen and pantry.

I found the number of the house I had been seeking. There was no name plate on the door, but I lifted the polished brass knocker and yanked it down to announce my presence. A few moments passed, and I wondered if anyone were home. Then the door swung open, and my breath caught. For there on the step stood the lady Genevieve la Chance!

I stood for a moment speechless, prey to conflicting emotions. The memory of our brief interlude on the train surged over me: her moving performance as an innocent newly-arrived immigrant, the bulky wallet of stolen bank notes thrust into my hands. I raised my hat and bowed to the lady.

"Madame!" I said.

"You, sir!" she exclaimed, her face colouring.

"Rest assured madame, I have not sought you out. My presence here is pure coincidence."

"Yes?"

Her breath came more quickly, and I could not help but fall again under her spell, that of the beautiful innocent creature needing help in a strange land.

"I am in fact seeking a young man . . ." I began.

"A young man?" She seemed surprised.

"A certain Reggie Braithwaite. I was given this address. His father, in London, wanted me to look him up. He has not heard from him."

The lady stood in the doorway for a moment longer, and looked at me with her clear grey eyes. Then she moved aside to allow me to enter.

"Perhaps you had better come in, sir!" she said.

It was a modestly well-to-do drawing room into which I was shown. Tastefully furnished, a comfortable divan and matching chair, upholstered in some grey material, a table with a vase of fresh flowers, a few well-chosen pictures on the walls. A pert Irish maid came in bearing a tea tray.

"Thank you, Bridget. Just put it down."

"Yes ma'am."

The tray was placed on the table between us, and the girl went out again, closing the door quietly behind her.

"You do know Reggie, then?" I queried.

"I came over from England to join him."

"You what?" I cried, the events of the past few days still vivid in my mind.

"But things do not always go according to plan."

I reined in my impatience. "May I ask what you mean, madame?"

She poured tea into the delicate Limoges cups. "I mean that there are as many rogues, in this part of the world, preying upon their less fortunate brethren, as there are in the worst slums and factory towns of Britain. Crossing the sea does not change human nature, sir," she said firmly.

I accepted a cup of tea.

"Surely you are not referring to your fiancé, Madame."

"Perhaps even him."

"Madame," I said after a moment, "you speak as if you had suffered at the hands of these rogues, as you describe them."

"Indeed I have, sir."

"And yet, I feel I must remind you, it was you who passed a hundred dollars in stolen bank notes in exchange for my gold sovereigns. An action which incidentally landed me in Kingston Penitentiary."

"That was not intended, I assure you."

She sipped her tea.

"I suppose it was not intended either, that I should have the misfortune to meet a lout of a man, who came looking for you after you had left the train. An American."

She looked up at me with sympathy.

"A rude fellow," I went on, "with a most threatening manner. I left him to go to the dining car, and upon my return I found him in my seat, apparently unconscious. I examined him. He was dead."

"Yes?"

"You don't seem surprised, madame, nor shocked."

"No, sir — only relieved."

I gazed at her in wonder. "Relieved, madame?"

The lady put down her teacup with a firm hand and confronted me. "Reggie Braithwaite — the man whom you seek — and I were childhood sweethearts. We grew up together. He travelled the world and decided that his future lay here in Canada. I was more than willing to share it with him. He wrote to me, telling of his plans, an offer of marriage and the promise of a fine estate in Ontario. He gave me the address of his agent in London, and under his auspices I took passage to Canada. On the ship, I was to meet a representative of the agent, an American gentleman who was en route to the United States via Ontario, where he had property of his own to dispose of, and who would at the same time look after my interests."

"Yes?"

"Suffice it to say, that this 'gentleman' proved to be a rascal, one of those who prey upon innocent newcomers to this country, particularly those of the fair sex."

She paused, brushing away angry tears.

"You speak as if with some authority, madame."

"I do indeed, sir," she replied. "My fiancé has disappeared. I have been caught up in a network of land fraud, gambling, and speculation. The government of Canada generously encourages immigration to this country, but there are those who would divert good and useful legitimate plans to their own unscrupulous purposes."

"Your agent was such a person?"

"He was, sir, and I became dependent on that evil man for my very life!"

"So you were not unduly concerned to learn of his demise?" I chose my words carefully.

"Frankly, sir, I was delighted," the lady replied in a firm voice. She sipped her tea.

I tried again. "Madame, I cannot help but be sympathetic, but I am puzzled how this matter relates to the stolen bank notes which you prevailed upon me to exchange."

"As I remember, you were quite willing to effect an exchange," she looked at me coolly. "One hundred dollars in notes for ten sovereigns in gold coin."

"I did not at the time realize that the bank notes were stolen," I said.

"So you were quite willing to make one hundred percent profit on your transaction, providing the money was good."

I gazed at her with dismay, remembering how I had viewed her on the train as a lady in distress; how she had pushed the wallet into my hands, unasked; how she had pressed against me, the touch of her lips on my cheek.

"Perhaps you would like your wallet back," I said. I took it from my pocket and opened it. "I'm afraid the authorities in Montreal kept the hundred dollars."

"Thank you," she said.

She made no effort to take it. Neither did she offer to return the sovereigns I had loaned her, so after a moment I closed the wallet and laid it gently on the table between us.

"I do not wish to intrude upon you further, madame," I said, rising. "I had hoped to find the Honourable Reggie Braithwaite at this address. . . ."

"He is not here, sir, and I do not know of his whereabouts. I am truly sorry; please forgive me."

She had risen and offered me her hand, which I took in mine for a moment. I raised it to my lips, conscious of her scented warmth. As if on a signal, the Irish maidservant appeared and showed me to the door. I had been royally dismissed.

I suppose I have met women like Genevieve la Chance before, or at least I have heard of them, women who, from whatever station of life, realize that their best opportunity lies in their beauty and their wits. Such women recognize a social structure in which men are encouraged to take advantage of any attractive women who cross their paths. The number of showgirls of humble origin who marry into leading families illustrates my point. These women often bring bright intelligence, maturity, and stamina into what at times appears to be a decaying British aristocracy.

Not that I would have thought Genevieve had her social origins on the stage, though the way she had beguiled me smacked of histrionics. Indeed, I found her hard to place. Here was a woman, seemingly unattached, who claimed to be a newly-arrived immigrant of the moneyed class, taking up land in rural Ontario with a man who in fact had disappeared — a woman who in point of fact was to all appearances well set up in a modest but fashionable part of Toronto, complete with a bright, intelligent, Irish housemaid.

As thus I mused, wondering whether to return to my hotel or to stroll through the pleasant environs in which I found myself, a cab drew up in front of the house I had just vacated. The door of the cab opened, and a fashionably dressed gentleman emerged from its interior.

He spoke to the driver. "Pick me up in an hour, will you George?"

"Very good, sir," said the driver. He clucked to his horse, and went off down the street. The gentleman pulled out a pocket watch to check the time, twirled the tips of his moustache, and adjusted the angle of his silk hat. He walked up to the door I had so recently left. It opened silently to let him in, then closed discreetly behind him.

Chapter VI
The Plot Thickens

When I returned to my hotel, in the lobby I found Sherlock Holmes seated comfortably in a brown-leather upholstered easy chair. Enveloped in a cloud of tobacco smoke, he was reading the morning newspaper. On the marble floor at his side, was what they call in this country a "spittoon." A spittoon — I mention this only in passing — is a curious vessel of polished brass, with flaring sides, about the size of a small chamber pot. It is provided for those hotel patrons who chew tobacco instead of smoking it, and who must relieve themselves periodically by expectorating.

"Hullo, Holmes," said I, taking a seat.

"Good morning, Watson," my friend replied, barely glancing in my direction. "How is the lady Genevieve this morning?"

I reined in my impatience. "What, Holmes, do you know of the lady Genevieve?"

"For one thing, she uses a perfume, *Eau de l'amour* if I'm not mistaken, of a particularly cloying characteristic."

"Good Lord!"

I lifted my fingers to my nose. It was faint, but unmistakable, that delightful, intriguing scent that had quickened my pulse.

"Further, she is living, at the moment, in a pleasant stone cottage on Yorkville Avenue, where she receives gentlemen callers, and where this morning you in fact paid her court, my dear Watson."

I looked at Holmes with mixed feelings. Was I to have no private life? And yet I knew that it was he who constantly provided for me the spice without which, perhaps, life would not be worth living. Also I knew that when the lady's door had closed upon me, and I was no closer to the riddle of the missing Reggie, I had longed for the guidance of my friend Sherlock Holmes.

"Were you following me, Holmes?" I asked.

"Good Lord, no! My dear fellow, that would be quite unethical!"

"I am pleased to hear that!" I said.

"Actually, I happened to pass the lady's establishment earlier this morning, and I noticed a fragrant yellow bush on the right side of the door. There is a trace of yellow pollen on your left sleeve, Watson. Pure coincidence, no doubt." He drew on his pipe for a moment. "As to gentlemen callers, I recognized a certain American diplomat, now stationed here in Toronto, who chose the moment of my passing to leave the lady's house, having no doubt dropped by to pay his cordial respects."

"Whatever you are inferring, Holmes, I assure you that my visit to the lady Genevieve was of the utmost propriety."

"My dear fellow, I am sure it was!"

"I was given that address to make contact with my friend's son, Reggie Braithwaite, about whom I told you. I was most surprised when confronted with the lady in question."

Holmes's pipe had gone out, and he leaned over to knock the dottle into the brass spittoon.

"And what did you learn of the whereabouts of your Reggie Braithwaite?"

"I learned nothing, Holmes. Although the lady claims she came to this country to marry this young man and to take up property in the vicinity of Niagara Falls, she seems at the moment to make no effort to find him."

"Curious," said my friend thoughtfully. "Have you any idea why that might be?"

"Holmes," I said in a burst of exasperation, "in my time, I have known many women. . . ."

"On three separate continents. You have mentioned that."

" . . . But I must admit that the fair sex continues to baffle me."

"Pity," said Holmes. "Knowing of your reputation in that department, I was hoping to elicit your assistance." So saying, my friend retired again behind his newspaper.

I did not know whether to be pleased or aggravated by Holmes's manner. From long association with him, I had come to realize that I felt truly alive only when I was in his company — one might say that I lived from one Sherlockian adventure to another. My professional medical practice in London was pushed aside with some frequency when "the game was afoot," and indeed my marriage to dear Mary Morstan was on more than one occasion interrupted by Holmes's demands and, I must admit it, my willing acquiescence to them.

"What would you have me do, Holmes?" I asked at length.

He thrust aside the newspaper and turned to me, eyes bright. "Good man!"

"That remains to be seen," I replied.

"But you are already in the midst of it, dear fellow!" he exclaimed. "The fortuitous meeting you had on the train with the lady Genevieve, the money she gave you, your unfortunate arrest and incarceration. . . ."

Patiently I took a deep breath. "Holmes," I said, "perhaps you would be good enough to tell me what is the context of all this?"

"There is reason to believe that your lady is a political agent," said Holmes.

"She's what?" I exclaimed.

"I have learned from my friend Hargreaves in New York that there are delicate matters now being negotiated between London and Washington with respect to certain aspects of Canadian sovereignty. As always, there are those who seek to turn political decisions to their own advantage, and will use any means to achieve their end."

"Including a beautiful woman with a grievance?" I said.

"Exactly!" exclaimed Holmes. "Even to providing the grievance if necessary."

"I don't follow you."

"The lady in question sails to this country from England, intending to marry her well-to-do childhood sweetheart and become a member of the landed gentry. Instead, abused and robbed by a rascally land agent, and seemingly deserted by her lover, she turns her not inconsiderable talents against the community, for whatever personal benefit and satisfaction she can derive."

"Yes. She told me some of that."

"Oh, she did."

Holmes seemed pleased and was about to continue, but broke off as a waiter approached, silver tray in hand. On the tray was an envelope. Holmes reached out a long white hand and took it.

"Ah!" he said. "Thank you."

He opened the envelope and read its contents.

"Very timely," said Holmes. "Be good enough to show him up to Doctor Watson's rooms in five minutes, would you?"

He put a few coins on the man's tray.

"Very good, sir," replied that worthy.

We had barely gained my quite comfortable rooms, when there was a discreet tap on the door. I opened it and was confronted by a stocky, middle-aged fellow wearing a brown mackintosh, a brown bowler hat, and an enormous brown walrus moustache. He thrust out a powerful hand and shook mine vigorously.

"Doctor Watson," he said. "*The* Doctor Watson!"

"Indeed, sir!" I replied, somewhat taken aback that he should know my identity.

"Inspector Maloney, Schenectady Police Department."

"Ah yes," said I.

"Maloney, do come in," said Holmes. The grip on my hand relaxed, and was transferred to Holmes's slender fingers. "Inspector Hargreaves wired me to expect you. We were just about to have a glass of sherry. Perhaps you will join us."

Our visitor entered the room, and I closed the door behind him.

"I have followed your adventures, Holmes, with considerable interest and pleasure," he said.

"You honour me, sir," replied Holmes. As I have noted before, Holmes was not entirely averse to praise. On occasion his normally sallow cheeks would flush under the stimulus of an appreciative word.

Our visitor removed his hat and mackintosh and, loosening his cravat, lowered himself comfortably into one of the easy chairs. "So you are the fellow that went over the Reichenbach Falls and was mourned as dead," Maloney observed as he accepted a glass of sherry.

"Officially sir, I am still dead," replied Holmes. "My corpse is somewhere down in that dreadful cauldron of swirling water and seething foam."

"That's what you might call really going under cover," remarked our guest in a droll fashion.

"That was the idea," said Sherlock Holmes. "Cheers!" He raised his glass.

"Your good health," replied Maloney. He half-emptied his glass at a gulp, and wiped his moustache with a blunt forefinger.

"I gathered from friend Hargreaves that you wished to seek my advice on a matter touching on British, Canadian, and American sovereignty," said Holmes.

"That's correct," said our visitor. He finished his glass. "Good stuff, that." I refilled it.

"I am informed that an American agent was recently found dead in a Canadian railroad train," said Maloney. "Somewhere between Quebec and Montreal. Hargreaves tells me that you may know something about it."

"Actually, I happened to be on the train at the time," said Holmes, "But I must admit that I was unaware of the presence of your agent."

"Well, our undercover guys are purty good," said our American visitor. He tossed back the sherry.

A match flared in Holmes's slender fingers. "Foul play?" he said, applying the flame to his pipe.

"Suspected. Not proven." Maloney reached for the decanter. "May I?"

"Yes, of course, dear fellow." Holmes exhaled a cloud of fragrant smoke, which he brushed aside with his hand. "You don't find my smoke bothersome, I trust."

"Not a bit," replied our visitor, refilling his glass. "I'll tell you about this Heindecker fellow. That was his name, Silas Heindecker."

Holmes nodded, relaxing in his easy chair, eyes closed in characteristic fashion.

"He'd been in London, and in Amsterdam. He came back to this continent by way of Quebec, routed to travel by train, first to Ottawa, then to Washington. He was reported as carrying with him certain highly confidential papers regarding the building of the Canadian Pacific Railway. There seems to have been misuse of funds, millions of dollars lining the pockets of certain unscrupulous people at the expense of the public. By the time Heindecker's body was in the hands of the Montreal Police, there was no sign of the papers. So I am told. It is safe to say they could compromise some of the more prominent names in the country."

"America or Canada?"

"Both, sir."

"The building of the railway was completed successfully, I take it," I interjected mildly.

"Oh yes, to strict deadlines. A magnificent achievement, through some of the world's most rugged territory."

"Well then?"

"My professional commitment lies not with the railway *per se*, but in the apprehension of the person or persons responsible for the death of the American Silas Heindecker, and the recovery, if possible, of the documents with which he had been entrusted."

Holmes puffed out a cloud of smoke. "Why approach me in this matter?" he said. "I am just a visitor here. Incognito. On holiday."

"Incognito, exactly!" cried Maloney. "Just what is needed! There are tensions between Washington, London and Ottawa at the present time, which it is thought would not be improved by an official investigation into the matter. I might also say that Hargreaves is personally keen on you, and has recommended you to the highest authorities in Washington."

Holmes flushed slightly, pleased as always at a professional tribute to his prowess. He leaned over the fireplace and knocked the ashes out of his dead pipe. He then turned back to our visitor.

"In that case, my dear Maloney, I can hardly refuse," said Sherlock Holmes.

Chapter VII
A Lady in Peril

As I have related elsewhere, my friend Holmes has an uncanny ability to observe, and to put together random clues which would escape the average intelligence, thus weaving a web of evidence to catch the wrongdoer. I have seen him fling himself to the ground, nostrils flaring like a hound on the scent, to scrutinize a bent blade of grass through his magnifying lens. In the dust of an empty attic, I have observed him discover and examine a footprint which led to the resolution of a murder case.

But this time he was undertaking to solve a mystery which no longer seemed to present useful evidence for his keen scrutiny.

It was doubly ironic, it seemed to me, that the death of the man Heindecker, whether by poison, the lethal bite of an exotic spider, or a combination of the two, should happen when Holmes had in fact been in an adjoining railway carriage, seemingly unaware of those events proceeding close by.

"By the way, Holmes."

"Yes, old boy?"

We were in a cab going west along Front Street, a thoroughfare which ran along the waterfront, busy with fishing boats, steam vessels, the active trade of a busy port.

"What the devil were you doing with that troupe of circus people, may I ask, with elephants and Bengal tigers?"

"Let us say I was entertaining my inexhaustible curiosity, Watson," said my companion, and with his stick he thumped the roof of the cab.

"Turn here, cabby," he said.

In response, the cab swung sharply in front of a heavily loaded dray and dodged a fish cart, its iron-shod wheels rattling over the cobbles.

"But to be in a railway carriage next door to a murder . . . " I began.

"Murder?" said my friend.

"Was it not murder?"

"That is what we are now engaged to determine," said Holmes. "I am informed that the number of the carriage where the unfortunate Heindecker met his end is CP 5692, and that the carriage is now at our disposal in the railway yard of this city, at the foot of York Street. We are on our way there now."

Presently a multiplicity of railway lines confronted us, gleaming in the light of the cold morning sun. White steam billowed from giant locomotives as they shunted from one track to another, patiently assembling freight and passenger cars into long trains, destined for who-knows-what distant part of this vast country.

An official-looking fellow in a flat cap and a brass-bound jacket turned towards us and raised his hand as we approached. Our cab pulled to a stop, the horses steaming in the September air.

"Do somethin' fer yez, gentlemen?" The accent was Irish.

"Where will we find car CP 5692?" queried Holmes.

"Oh, yes," said the fellow, "I wuz told to expect yez. She's on the siding down there, off to one side."

He pointed us on our way, and in response our cabby clucked up his horses and we lurched down the cinder track which lay between the steel rails and the shunting engines.

The railway car that we sought lay seemingly abandoned, and as we climbed on board we felt the handrails gritty with an accumulation of the all-pervasive soot from the nearby locomotives. Unlike the English railway carriage more familiar to me, the Canadian counterpart has only two exterior doors, one at either end, through one of which we now entered.

Inside the unheated carriage it was cold, and our breath hung in the dead air. I shivered in spite of myself, as I once more confronted the seat I had occupied on my trip from Quebec, and where such dramatic scenes had been played out. I glanced down the carriage. It was silent and empty, and I wondered for a moment to what far-flung destinations my fellow immigrants had disappeared.

"I take it that this is the seat you occupied, Watson?"

Holmes's voice broke into my thoughts. My companion was already intent on the task for which he had come.

"That's correct, Holmes, until I went forward to the dining car."

"And the lady?"

"She was in the corner there facing me."

Holmes was on his knees, looking under the seats, with that curious intensity which overcomes him at such times. Suddenly, with a grunt, he reached back into his pocket for his magnifying glass, and then lay on his stomach on the inhospitable floor, wriggling half under the seat in his effort.

I could hear him muttering to himself for a minute or two, and then he backed out, his usually pale face flushed with exasperation.

"Dash it all, Watson," he burst forth, "the railway company was instructed to put the car on the siding for examination, but it would seem they didn't inform their cleaning staff. The whole carriage is as clean as a new pin! It reeks of disinfectant. It should have been sealed off at once!"

Thus releasing his frustration, my friend set to again, painstakingly going over every inch of the two seats which had experienced such dramatic events.

As I watched him, I conjured up the vision of the beauty which had met my eyes upon first boarding the train. I even thought I could detect faint traces of the beguiling perfume she wore. That was absurd of course; the place, as Holmes had remarked, now reeked of disinfectant.

"Where did this fellow sit — Heindecker?" demanded Holmes.

"He occupied the lady's seat, after she had left the train," I replied.

"Show me!" said my companion.

Obligingly, I took up the position in which I remembered Heindecker. "His bag was here," I said. "From it he took half a chicken and a bottle of wine."

"And on your return from the dining room?"

"He was slumped across like this." I demonstrated. "As if in a drunken stupor. I had difficulty in getting past him into my own seat."

"And his bag?"

"It was still there."

"Open or closed?"

"Open. I closed it."

"Did you search the bag before you closed it?"

"No, I didn't, Holmes."

"Just as well," he grunted.

"Why?"

"With a deadly spider in it?"

"Yes, of course! By Jove!"

I got out of Holmes's way as, peering intently through his magnifying glass, he patiently examined the crevices between the stiff horsehair seat cushions. There was nothing to be found, or perhaps the cleaners had done their job too well. Then suddenly he paused, and from his pocket he took a pair of medical tweezers, with which he retrieved something I could not quite see.

"What is it, Holmes?"

"A hair."

"Oh?"

"A particular hair, Watson. Light brown in colour. Wiry in texture. An animal hair, I think, rather than human."

With a thoughtful air he put away the magnifying glass, and transferred the solitary hair into an envelope he produced from his pocket. He marked the envelope and put it away, looked pensively around the carriage, then with a suddenness that quite startled me, he sprang to his feet.

"Come, Watson!" he cried. "We are in the wrong place."

He moved swiftly out of the train, and in a moment we had regained our cab, driver and horses waiting patiently for us amidst the railway tracks and the shunting steam engines.

"National Exhibition Grounds at all speed, driver!"

The cab took off with such rapidity that I perforce was obliged to hold onto the straps provided for such occasions.

"We have been diverted, Watson! Examining a railway carriage, newly-cleaned, while the plot lies elsewhere!"

It was not long before we regained Front Street, and west of Bathurst came upon an open field in which colourful tents had been recently erected. There were show booths, a roundabout, and all the signs of a country fair. Horse-drawn tramcars disgorged crowds of excited youngsters and patient mothers, carrying picnic baskets in preparation for a day's outing. There was the distinctive sound of a steam calliope, that ingenious offspring of the barrel organ. Its melody carried on the fresh breeze from the lake, and mingled with the shouts of barkers and shills crying their wares.

Holmes dismissed the cab, and we entered the fairgrounds in some haste. The air smelled of crushed grass, roasted peanuts, candy floss and horse dung. Barkers shouted with hoarse voices above the babel of the throng, promising everything from "life-enhancing patent medicines," to the "thrill of a lifetime," the latter seemingly only possible upon payment of a fee which entitled the unwary customer to go behind one of a series of lurid canvas screens, on which were painted two-headed monsters with dripping fangs, midgets and extravagantly shaped females.

There were "spin the wheel" devices where the customer had little chance of winning any more than a token celluloid doll clothed in pink feathers. There were stands where one shied hard balls at a target, and if accurate, thereby dumped a clown into a tub of water. High-spirited visitors out for a good time, beaming faces sticky with candy floss and toffee apples, loved it all.

"What are we doing here, Holmes?" I ventured.

Holmes made no reply, other than to quicken his pace. As we approached the end of the Midway, the atmosphere subtly changed. There was a tangible quality of danger in the air, an acrid smell I associated with India. I saw Holmes's nostrils dilate as he lifted his head, and his grey eyes sharpened. A great circus tent faced us, and somewhere behind the canvas, a tiger snarled.

We went to the box office. Then, tickets in hand, we joined the high-spirited holiday crowd entering the enclosure.

". . . a show was already in progress . . ."
(Sitting Bull and Buffalo Bill)

In a sawdust ring, enclosed by a low wooden barricade, a show was already in progress, with bareback Red Indian riders circling at a gallop in a dazzling display of horsemanship, at one moment standing erect on the rumps of their swiftly moving steeds, the next swinging themselves under the horses' bellies. The warriors had bows and arrows, and strove each to outdo the other in marksmanship, shooting their arrows with remarkable accuracy at a target set up at the end of the arena.

Holmes and I had found ourselves seats so close to the barricade that the thump of horses' hooves, the exhalation of their breath, the very sweat on the brown skins of the warriors became almost palpable, and the energy and swiftness with which the bows were drawn and the arrows fired, keyed up my sense of anticipation and danger.

As the warriors galloped off, applause turned to laughter as a pair of clowns rushed out, shovels in hand, to make a great to-do scooping up horse manure, real or imagined, that had been left behind. Simultaneously, three slender figures, two men and a woman, glittering in abbreviated spangled costumes, climbed a rope ladder leading to the high wire, which stretched across the roof of the tent, from one pole to another, supported by guy ropes.

A kettledrum rolled, and tension in the audience increased. I was aware of Holmes shifting uneasily in his seat, the better to see the coming action, or perhaps sensing danger.

The shining figures, high above the crowd, reached a small platform at one end of the taut wire, and in a moment one of the men had seized a trapeze bar in his hands, and had swung out high over the heads of the audience. There was a gasp from the latter, as in mid-air the acrobat released his hold and dived headlong to grasp a second bar upon which again he swung with great vigour before letting go, and, turning a somersault in mid-air, landed like a cat on another platform at the far end of the wire.

Now the second bespangled artist took the trapeze in hand and flew in a great arc high above the sawdust floor. At the height of his swing, he adroitly reversed his position, so that he now hung by his feet, and as he swung back, arms free, his hands were outstretched to grasp those of the lady waiting on the platform. With impeccable timing the manoeuvre was accomplished, and as the hands of the aerial acrobats came together, the lady launched herself from her perch as gracefully as any bird in flight.

I became conscious then of an additional element in the drama being enacted high above me. The acrobat and the lady were in mid-flight, curving in a wide arc, he hanging by his heels from the trapeze, and she gripping his hands. But one of the tall masts between which the aerial apparatus was suspended seemed to be bending, and in consequence the high wire was losing its tension. There were cries of dismay from the audience as it became apparent that the whole thing was in danger of collapsing, thus endangering the lives of the performers.

The acrobats had swung to the second trapeze with such timing that the lady had already relinquished the support of her fellow performer, and had reached for the next bar to swing to the safety of the far platform. Her slender hands gripped the bar, and she flew like a bird through the intervening space. But the sagging mast and guy ropes retarded her action, and it seemed that the shining figure was going to fall short of its target and be dashed to the ground. At the peak of the swing, the lady let go of the trapeze and, turning in mid-air, took the outstretched hands of her fellow acrobat already waiting for her, perched precariously on his platform. In a moment she was safely beside him, turning and bowing to the cheering crowd before sliding down the pole to safety. As she did so, the supporting ropes parted, and the whole rig came crashing down into the sawdust.

The dust had barely cleared before Holmes was over the barrier and into the ring. The audience, curious as to what had happened, was being shown out of the tent in good order.

"What do you make of this, Watson?"

I found Holmes peering through his glass at the ragged end of a broken hemp rope.

"The guy rope broke under excessive strain," I said.

"Look more closely!" Holmes jabbed at the broken fibres with a long forefinger. "Those fibres in the centre."

Without waiting for my answer, he thrust the broken rope end into my hands, and dropped to his knees in the sawdust, sniffing about for all the world like a hound on the trail. He examined the top of the wooden barrier where the rail had been worn smooth by constant abrasion of some sort. Beyond the barrier, coiled upon itself like some kind of evil snake, the rope fed through a system of pulleys, which, shackled to a great iron ring embedded in concrete, enabled the circus crew to put the necessary tension on the high wire.

"It doesn't appear to be cut, Holmes," I said. "Perhaps a bit discoloured at the point of the break."

Holmes turned to me again, and virtually snatched the rope out of my hand, and with his pocketknife he cut a few fibres from the rope at the point of the break. These he thrust into an envelope which then disappeared into a capacious inner pocket. Holmes, for some reason, was not in a good mood.

I was conscious of the approach of Flaherty, the circus entrepreneur, bowler hat at an angle, his blue eyes worried.

Behind him, at a discreet distance, I observed the Andaman pygmy, Jo-Jo, who seemed alert and watchful. To my surprise, Flaherty ignored Holmes and came directly to me.

"Doctor Watson! Nice to see you again, sorr." His Irish brogue was warm. "Did ye see the accident?"

"I did," I said. "I trust no one was hurt."

"The lady is shaken up a bit."

"I'm sorry to hear that."

"In fact since you're here, sorr, I would appreciate your coming backstage and taking a look at her."

"Right," said I.

Flaherty turned, and I shot a glance at Holmes, who, ignoring us, was strolling away in the opposite direction like any idle sightseer. I remembered the scene I had witnessed in the railway carriage, with Holmes in his role as Hindu snake charmer, performing under Flaherty's very nose. Holmes evidently had not revealed his true identity then, and presumably he did not wish to now.

I followed Flaherty across the ring. Members of the company, some still in costume, were already untangling the wires and ropes, preparing to remount the aerial rig. Jo-Jo's monkey scampered across the floor avoiding the wreckage, and leaped onto the pygmy's shoulder.

"The show must go on," I said to my escort.

"Indeed, sorr," he replied. "In the best tradition of the circus. Though, at times, I must say I wonder."

"What do you mean?"

"Well, one day it's a tiger on the loose. Another day, a perfectly sound hemp rope breaks. People's lives are threatened. It was a miracle that my lady aerialist was not dashed to the ground."

"Indeed," I replied.

"We're going to be packing up in a day or two, anyway," said Flaherty. "Going to Niagara Falls, all being well. We'll attract a good crowd there. After that, we go to the States."

Beyond the canvas curtains of the ring, we entered another world, where animals and human beings from diverse sources lived and worked together in harmony, mutually dependent. Exotic animals were being groomed and fed, and in a outdoor kitchen, food was being prepared for the human members of the troupe.

Flaherty led me to one of a number of caravans and tapped on the door. I heard a female voice from within.

"Yes?"

Flaherty pushed open the door and thrust his head inside. "I've brought a doctor to look at you, milady." Thus announcing his purpose, the good fellow stood aside and motioned me to enter. I squeezed past him into the caravan. There before me on a *chaise longue*, wrapped in an attractive *peignoir*, was Genevieve la Chance!

Chapter VIII
A Chemical Experiment

Back in my hotel, I retrieved the key to my room, and the desk clerk handed me a folded slip of paper.

"Message, sir."

"Thank you." I read the note: "Checked in Rm 212 w'd apprec. visit. H."

Room 212 was next to mine. I tapped on the door, and it swung open to reveal Sherlock Holmes in his shirt sleeves. An acrid odour hung in the air.

"Ah, Watson! You are just in time," said Holmes. "I am in the process of conducting a modest chemical analysis."

On a deal table near the window was a lighted Bunsen burner fed by a slender rubber tube from the room's gas fixture. Above the burner, held by a metal clamp, was a glass retort, in which bubbled an inch or so of clear liquid. Upon the floor under the table lay two discarded cardboard boxes, in which presumably the apparatus had been delivered. Two or three small bottles of chemicals stood on the table. Holmes had wasted no time.

From his pocket my friend now retrieved the envelope I had seen him place there earlier in the day. He opened it with his long fingers, and upended it over the retort. A few wispy bits of hemp rope fell into the bubbling liquid, which then slowly turned blue.

"Just as I thought," said Sherlock Holmes.

He smiled with satisfaction, ignited a spill of paper at the Bunsen flame, and with it lit his worn briar pipe. In a moment he was enveloped in a cloud of *habitant* tobacco smoke.

"I have taken quite a liking to this Canadian tobacco," he said.

"So I have noticed."

I could not refrain from coughing, and I waved away the smoke with my hand.

"Not to your taste, Watson?" He seemed amused at my discomfort.

I sat down in one of the room's two chairs, while Holmes returned to his chemical apparatus. He turned off the gas jet, and the flame of the Bunsen burner vanished with a pop, the fluid in the glass beaker ceased to bubble.

"And how is the lady Genevieve?" he queried.

"Good Lord, Holmes!" I exclaimed. "I had no idea it was she until I was escorted into her dressing room."

"She's alive and well then, I take it?"

"Yes, yes, indeed she is."

Holmes nodded towards his chemical experiment. "Hydrochloric acid," he said. "Enough to weaken the high wire guy ropes to the point of breaking under additional strain. The lady is indeed fortunate to be alive, and I blame myself in the matter."

"An accident, Holmes?"

"It would be difficult to prove otherwise, Watson," Holmes replied. "I must tell you I have been keeping my eye on her movements for some weeks. Indeed it was for that purpose I was on the train where you discovered me, and where the man we now know to be the American agent Heindecker met his unfortunate end."

"Surely you are not suggesting. . . ."

". . . That the lady had anything to do with Heindecker's demise?" Holmes's voice was sharp. "You were there, Watson. What do *you* think?"

"She left the train before he came on board," I said.

"Exactly," said Holmes, his brow furrowed with frustration.

"The lady is a remarkable person," I ventured.

"Too jolly remarkable, in my opinion," snapped Holmes.

"She was confiding in me — " I said.

"Oh, was she indeed!" my companion regarded me coldly. "And what did she have to say, pray?"

"Since you ask me, Holmes," I said. "She was born in the Cockney slums of London, and pulled herself out of that limited environment by her own effort, talent, and intelligence. She became an outstanding actress in London and in Paris. She speaks English and French beautifully, and she could now hold her own on any level of society, if I am any judge!"

"Exactly," said Holmes. "One who can mix at any level of society, and one more than ever determined in the pursuit of her goal."

"Her goal, Holmes?"

"She has the power to disrupt world affairs."

"Travelling with a circus?" I said incredulously. "Surely not!"

"A circus is like a family, Watson, a mutually protective community. One, moreover, that is able to move at will, and to cross international boundaries with little formality or question. Furthermore, you may be sure that after the 'accident' that we witnessed today, enclosed in that mutually protective group, no stranger will get anywhere near her for any purpose, unless she wishes it!"

". . . an excellent railway service . . ."

Chapter IX
The Body in the Swamp

The following morning, in the hotel lobby, as I went into breakfast, a newsboy thrust a newspaper at me.

"Extra! Read all about it! Body in the Swamp! Paper, sir?"

I gave the boy a coin, he tucked the folded paper neatly under my arm, and I went into the dining room. Holmes was already seated, his back to the wall, behind a corner table. He was picking at a plate of ham and eggs, a book of some sort on the table before him. His concentration was such that I did not disturb him. Rather, I ordered breakfast from the pert waitress, before unfolding the newspaper and perusing its contents. I must have uttered an exclamation, because Holmes looked up from his book.

"What are you grunting about?" he demanded.

"An item here in the newspaper."

"Yes?"

"The body of a young fellow, English upper class by his clothing, was found face down in a swamp. Two local fellows were returning home from a pig-butchering."

Holmes looked at me sharply. "Where was this?"

"A sparsely populated area in the vicinity of Woodfield, Ontario. The fellows who discovered the body were drunk, and bloody from their day's work. The authorities are holding them."

"Have they identified the victim?" Holmes was suddenly alert.

"Seemingly not. His pocket book is missing, and any identifying labels have been cut from his clothing."

The waitress arrived with my ham and eggs, toast, and coffee. I passed the newspaper over to Holmes, and poured myself a cup. Holmes looked at the paper for a few moments. I had no sooner cut into my ham and eggs than he was on his feet, pulling on his coat and calling the waitress for his bill.

"There is an excellent railway service from Union Station within the hour, which will take us to the location of this affair. I suggest we take it!"

He paid the wide-eyed waitress for his breakfast, flung a wool scarf around his neck, and pulled on his black velour hat. Though I am used to my friend's mercurial tendencies, he continues to surprise me. When he is in such a mood, I can but fall in with his wishes. Holmes did allow me to finish my breakfast, and in a short time we found ourselves once again in a Canadian railway train. This time, unlike the transcontinental, it was a modest local, which gave good service to the people of Ontario, both city and country, running on a dependable, frequent schedule from Toronto north to the Georgian Bay.

As we cleared the city this most raw and unseasonable day, there were dark clouds overhead, and the threat of snow in the air. Indeed, rattling through the sparsely populated countryside, we saw blown snow already accumulating in the ditches, and on the windward side of trees.

No more than an hour out of Toronto, we pulled into the small station of Woodfield, the nearest point to the bucolic swamp in which the tragic affair had taken place. We got off the train, and a penetrating northeast wind pounced upon us, blowing eddied gusts of fine snow around the corner of the modest station house. I pulled up my collar, wishing I were more warmly prepared for this adventure. Holmes wrapped his long woollen scarf more securely about his neck, and looked up and down the platform as the train puffed into the distance.

There was a creaking sound nearby, and the door in the station house swung open. "G'day," said a voice.

Holmes looked around. "And a good day to you!" he called out.

There was a pause, and the cold wind gusted about our ankles. The train hooted in the distance, and in the absence of further communication we moved over to the half-open door.

"Do anything fer youse fellas?"

The voice sounded Irish to me, unused as I yet was to the accents of rural Ontario.

Inside the station house, in the warmth of a glowing potbellied stove, stood a small man in his shirt sleeves, iron-grey hair standing on end, and a day's stubble of beard on his chin. He viewed us without curiosity. There was a kettle boiling on the stove.

"C'mon in and shut the door."

He had taken some mugs from a shelf, and was placing them on a table near the stove, along with a bottle of Holland gin, a tin tablespoon, and a cracked cup half full of brown sugar.

"Boiling water," he said. "Sugar and gin. Keeps out the cold." He dished up the mixture. "Have some," he said. "It cures what ails yer."

"Very decent of you, I'm sure," said Holmes, accepting a steaming mug of the mixture.

"Thank you," said I. "Very welcome."

"My pleasure," said the little man, and he blew on his drink to cool it.

"If you've come to see the body, you're too late. They took it away," he went on.

"Where did they take it?"

"Elmville. Just up the line. Funeral parlour. You'd be surprised the number of people come to see the body of a fellow human being after he's dead. Particularly after he's been murdered."

He sipped his drink with obvious relish. "If it's too hot, ye can put some more gin in it," he offered. "Cool it down."

"No, this is fine," said Holmes. "He was murdered, then?"

"Oh, right enough. They took in the fellas that did it. Been cuttin' up pigs. Still had their knives with them. Covered with blood."

"Pig's or human?"

"How can you tell? Fellas from up the line a piece. Stinkin' drunk they was!" Our host emptied most of his cup at a draught.

"So there is nothing now to be seen in the swamp?"

"Lots of footprints. Few spots of blood, maybe. With this snow coming on, you won't see much."

"Where was he from?"

"The dead feller?"

"Yes."

"Oh, a stranger. Good lookin' young feller. Good clothes. Nice pair of shoes. Don't know where from, though. That's why they got 'im laid out up there. Identification. Hundreds of people've come by to look at 'im."

"Did he come in on the train?"

"Sure he come on the train. Two of them. Just like you fellers. The dead feller had an English accent."

"And the other?"

"Didn't hear his voice. They walked up the road there, and that's the last I saw."

"So the other fellow didn't come back either."

"Nope. He could've walked a few miles to the next station down the line, and taken the train from there back to where they come from."

"And where did they come from?"

Our host raised his cup, and gulped the last of his drink, eyeing us as he did so.

"That's a good question," he said finally, putting down the empty cup, and wiping his mouth on the back of his hand. "Have you fellers finished yer drink?"

"Yes, thank you."

"Very warming."

"Glad you enjoyed it. That'll be fifty cents. Each."

Holmes and I exchanged glances. We fished in our pockets, and found the requested contribution.

"And where did you say these fellows had come from?" said Holmes, money in hand.

"I didn't," replied our host.

"Well then" — Holmes handed over the dollar — "where *did* they come from?"

"Their tickets was issued in Niagara Falls."

As good luck would have it, a horse and cart caught us on the road, and pulled up at our hail. The rough-looking driver looked us over.

"Fifty cents," he said.

"What?"

"I figger you fellers want to see the place where the feller got murdered. I'll take you there for fifty cents. Each."

"It seems to be a standard rate," said Holmes, who must have been quite as cold as I was.

"Use of the buffalo robe in back there for ten cents."

"Very decent of you, I'm sure," said Holmes, climbing into the back of the cart.

I clambered in beside him, and between us we shared the welcome warmth of the evil-smelling robe made of skins of buffalo — that noble animal which used to roam the Western plains in such vast numbers, and is now sadly reduced with the onset of our civilization.

The man spoke to his horse, and in a moment we were moving down the narrow road, the dark trees closing in around us, a strip of leaden sky above. The sound of our passage was curiously subdued by the sombre wall of trees, and when our driver spoke again, his voice was quiet in the presence of the dark forest.

"I'll wait fer youse, then I'll take you to the village. You can see the body at the undertaker's, and maybe catch a bit of something to eat with a glass of beer, at the tavern, before youse catch the train back to Toronto. It makes a nice outing."

"It sounds as if you're running a business here," said Holmes.

"A feller's got to take it as it comes, eh? I'm makin' enough out of this murder to tide me and my family over the winter. People's morbid curiosity."

I don't know where he learned the phrase, but it was true enough.

The trees thinned out presently, and the lowering sky became more evident as the dark pine forest gave way to a sparse growth of cedar and dead birch trees. Beside the road, between snow-covered tussocks of weedy growth, there appeared patches of open water, stagnant pools the colour of lead, reflecting the heavy overcast sky.

"Whoa!" cried the driver, and we lurched to a stop.

In the resulting silence, I could hear the horse breathing from his exertions, his breath turning to vapour on the frosty air.

"In there — you'll see where it's all tramped down. There's a stump with blood on it. I'll wait fer youse. . . . Don't know you'll see much. Blood on a stump."

We climbed stiffly from the cart, and the chilly wind met us again. The branches of such trees as there were in this remote swamp were rimed with hoarfrost, and I was aware that my breath was turning to ice in my moustache.

I wished again that Holmes had been decent enough to let me find myself a warm jacket before we set out from Toronto. I stepped tentatively onto the half-frozen sedge along the roadside, which crackled and oozed under my feet. Holmes was already ahead of me, in that curious state of concentration which comes over him on such occasions. He appears at once to close his mind from everyday associations, and to focus himself in areas of consciousness denied lesser beings. Certainly, his powers of sight and smell, of deduction and intuition, seem to me on occasion the stuff I have glimpsed among primitive tribesmen such as the Australian bushmen, and, I suppose, the North American Indians, though I myself have had little contact with the latter.

Suffice it to say that while I was tentatively picking my way across this miserable bog, wondering moment to moment whether I would slip and fall in, my companion had moved with certainty over the frozen tussocks to the bloody stump which marked the scene of the crime, and was already busy with magnifying glass, close to the ground, sniffing and muttering to himself, as if from the mist and the dank pools he would conjure up both victim and killer in tangible shape.

The ground in the vicinity of the stump, though now covered with light snow, was indented with scores of footprints, undoubtedly from the many sightseers who had come out of curiosity to view the tragic scene, as well as the officers of the law who reclaimed the body.

Holmes took out his penknife and scraped some of the dark substance from the stump, placing it in an envelope and labelling it. Then he moved wider in his investigation, peering under the stunted cedars and the snow-covered weeds and bushes. From time to time he would crouch down and, turning over the snowy leaves, retrieve some item too small for me to identify. He would make a notation in his pocket notebook, grunting the while, before moving on.

At one point, some twenty feet or so from the stump, he froze quite still, his gaze directed at a ragged branch of hawthorn which, at shoulder height, had interrupted his progress.

"See here, Watson!" His voice was sharp.

I squelched through the half-frozen mud, and peered through his lens.

"I see nothing, Holmes. A white mark on the branch, perhaps."

"Exactly. A thorn has been torn away." I moved slightly, shifting my position to see better. "Careful of the footprints, Watson! There are some under the snow!" He virtually barked at me.

I got out of his way, and Holmes crouched. With his fingertips he brushed aside the covering of snow, and in a moment gave a cry of satisfaction. There, half-buried in the trampled earth and fallen leaves, was a pair of spectacles. One of its lenses was broken. Holmes took up the glasses and examined them.

"To whom did these belong, Watson, do you suppose? To the murderer, or to his victim? Or to yet another?"

Carefully, he wiped the snow from the damaged glasses, and put them away in an inner pocket.

"Come along, Watson! It's time to find this 'tavern,' as the man calls it. Perhaps they can give us a hot gin!"

We picked our way out of that miserable place, leaving it to the muskrats and the horned owls.

In the village of Elmville, outside the undertaker's house, tended by the local constable, was a line of perhaps ten or a dozen people waiting in the cold. I glanced ahead and saw a familiar figure.

"I say, Holmes. . . ."

But my friend had already anticipated me. He went directly to the man I had spotted.

"Hullo, Maloney. A bit far from home, aren't you?"

"Holmes! I thought you might turn up."

It was Inspector Maloney, Schenectady Police Department, brown derby and all. He glanced at Holmes's muddy boots.

"You've been in the swamp," he said.

"Yes, actually," replied Holmes.

"Find anything?" Maloney peered at Holmes, squinting through the smoke from his stogie.

"The ground had been walked over."

"That's what I noticed."

"Oh, you were there?"

"Professional curiosity, like yourself."

"Quite," said Holmes. "And since we are here, I thought we might have a look at the body. Professional curiosity."

"Everybody else has. People from all over. Trying to identify him."

"Any success?"

"No."

The body lay there in the undertaker's, the face a curious wax-like bronze colour, fair hair, a slight stubble of beard, which from certain angles gleamed golden under the lamps. People in ones and twos, solemn, awe-struck, came in and viewed the still figure with a curious mixture of excitement and fear. That such a well dressed young man, handsome even in death, should be struck down in his prime without apparent cause, by an unknown assailant, must have been a reminder to the onlookers of the fleeting nature of life. The males removed their hats, the ladies dabbed their eyes, and if anyone spoke it was in subdued and reverent tones.

Presently we were alone in the place with Maloney and the body. The constable locked the door and stood by.

"What do you think, Holmes?" queried Maloney.

"I see that someone has taken the trouble to remove any identifying marks from the clothing, tailor's labels and so on. He has also removed any pocketbook, papers, letters, or anything which would identify the victim. The victim's clothing is expensive English tweed, with the characteristic cut of Bond Street. He wears a good English Burberry, light for the present inclement weather. And excellent handmade shoes — Josiah Carter's work, if I am not mistaken.

"An outdoor man, slender, but well-muscled. The well-kept hands are those of a gentleman. There is a thickening of the skin on portions of the fingers, a condition not uncommon to those who habitually ride horseback, and who handle the reins in either the English fashion or the American cowboy manner. His is characteristic of the English rider.

"Death appears to have been instantaneous by a small calibre bullet to the back of the head at close range. Such examination of the site of the murder as I was able to conduct would rule against a violent struggle between the deceased and his opponent. The evidence would therefore indicate that the victim was familiar with his assailant, if not friendly, and went willingly into that dismal swamp, where he met his tragic end. The latter, after shooting his companion to death, stripped his victim's clothing of identifying marks and disappeared, probably boarding the train at the next station down the line, to avoid recognition."

Holmes had pulled out his clay pipe, and was busy filling it. In a moment a wax vesta flared, and he exhaled clouds of smoke into the air. "The station master tells me that the two of them had return tickets to Niagara Falls. With one of them lying here before us, one might presume that the other, in fact, did return to that noble cataract."

He drew again on his pipe, then looked down his thin nose at our companion. "I wonder, my dear Maloney, if I may ask what your interest in this affair might be? You are, after all, an American detective, and here we are in Canada."

"As to that, Holmes, I need hardly point out that Niagara Falls is a border-crossing point between Canada and the United States," replied Maloney. "Niagara is, of course, a remarkable natural phenomenon, the eighth wonder of the world. It is also a nest of vipers, confidence men and tricksters. It is a place where, by simply walking across the suspension bridge, a person can move with ease from one country to another, on whatever dubious business he may have in mind. Part of my job, Holmes, is to keep an eye on such traffic."

While thus discoursing, Maloney had pulled out an imposing Longine pocket watch. He snapped open the cover and peered at its face. "We've just got time to see the pig stickers before the train comes in," he said.

"Pig stickers?" queried Holmes.

"In the local gaol. They're holding the guys that found the body. There's some doubt about the blood on their pants. Pig's blood or human?" He grinned as if he had just cracked a joke. He snapped his watch shut and was about to return it to his pocket.

"A fine Longine railway watch, is it not?" said Holmes, observing the action.

"Yes, indeed," said Maloney. "Presented to me by my grateful employers."

He held the timepiece up for Holmes's inspection. Holmes took it in his hand for a moment. "Very nice indeed. Fine workmanship. You're employed by the railway, then?" Holmes clicked the watch shut, and returned it to its owner.

"In a manner of speaking," replied our companion. "When it's mutually useful, you might say."

He had put away his timepiece and produced one of his stogie cigars. He placed it in his mouth, lit it, and in a moment was exuding clouds of foul-smelling smoke. Then the fellow tilted his brown derby hat at an angle that might have been termed "rakish" in a more debonair personality, and, nodding to the constable to unlock the door, left the room.

Holmes made as if to follow Maloney, but under the guise of pausing to adjust his scarf, he took the glasses he had retrieved from the swamp, and set them on the dead eyes and the rigid nose of the pale corpse that lay before us. As Holmes loosed his hold on the glasses, they slid sideways on the dead face, in a gross parody of lifelike motion. It was quite apparent that the spectacles did not belong to the dead man. Holmes took them up again and replaced them in his pocket. A moment later we rejoined Maloney in the darkening street.

Chapter X
The Guaiacum Test

"I must say, Watson, that I very much miss our snug quarters in Baker Street," said Sherlock Holmes.

He was at his table, taking notes from two or three books he had borrowed from the Osgoode Hall library that morning. Smoking his clay pipe, surrounded with test tubes, retorts, and glass tubing, as far as appearances go he might never had left London.

"What I would like is a plate of liver and bacon, with mashed potatoes, and a pint of good English beer."

He set out two petri dishes to carry out some kind of experiment.

"Speaking of Baker Street, Watson, how was our dear landlady when you saw her last?"

"Very much troubled, Holmes, to hear of your supposed demise in the Reichenbach Falls. She was one of those many Londoners who wore a black band in mourning for your loss. She still doesn't know the truth of the affair."

I am truly sorry about the whole Reichenbach business," said Holmes. "But it was necessary, you must acknowledge."

My friend was unusually loquacious, I thought. There are times when his customary cold exterior drops away, and reveals a surprising sensitivity for the feelings of others.

From a capacious pocket Holmes produced two envelopes, and from each of them, into the petri dishes, he
poured a few grains of a brownish powder, labelling one
"A," the other "B." He took a glass pipette in his fingers and
from it deposited a few drops of clear liquid onto the
powder, which then dissolved and took on the colour and the
texture of blood.

As I watched, he took another pipette and added a few
drops of some murky liquid to the mixture in the petri
dishes. Little change was evident.

"That's the saline solution, and the guaiacum," said
Holmes. "Now two drops of hydrogen dioxide."

"The guaiacum test," I said.

"Exactly," replied Holmes.

"I read of it in a recent medical journal. It appears quite
conclusive," I remarked.

"More than one innocent man has been wrongly con-
victed of murder because of incorrect identification of so-
called blood stains. The guaiacum test demonstrates whether
a given substance is indeed blood, and if so, when examined
under a microscope, blood of a human being or that of an
animal," responded Holmes.

"Thank God for the advances of medical science," I said
earnestly.

Holmes pointed to each of the petri dishes with a long
forefinger. "'A' is the substance I scraped from the stump,
where the swamp murder is said to have taken place. 'B' is
from the trouser leg of one of the poor fellows in the
Elmville gaol."

My friend took a fresh pipette in hand, and with it
deposited two drops of hydrogen dioxide on each of the petri
dishes. The effect was instantaneous; the bloody contents of
the dishes turned blue.

"So," said Holmes, putting the used pipette back into its rack. "We know it is blood. But is it human or animal?"

He took two microscope plates, and prepared them for viewing, recording the identity of each of the two smears of the bloody mixture.

"The blood corpuscle of the human being," said Holmes, "is one thirty-two-hundredth of an inch in diameter, I am informed. That seems to be unique amongst the warm-blooded creatures on this earth."

It has always amused me, when, from time to time, Holmes carries on like this. After all, I am the one with a degree in medicine.

"Animals with larger blood corpuscles than man range from the elephant to the great anteater and the platypus; with smaller, you have the porcupine, the kangaroo and the guinea pig." He glanced up at me. "Perhaps I could write a small paper on the subject, Watson!"

Thus he rattled on in a most jovial fashion, while setting up the microscope he had obtained somewhere, and sliding the prepared plates under the lens for viewing. Presently, he fell silent, peering into the eyepiece, and adjusting the focus. The only sound in the room was from liquid bubbling in the retort over the Bunsen burner.

"This one, 'A,' from the stump in the swamp," said Holmes at last, "is indeed human."

"And 'B'?" I asked.

Holmes changed the slides, and again adjusting the microscope, gazed into the eyepiece for fully a minute.

"Pig's blood!" said Sherlock Holmes.

The results of Holmes's diagnosis, we were to learn later, rather upset certain local town folk in Elmville, Ontario, who already had their minds made up on the matter. Some of them, in fact, were already looking forward to a public double hanging, which would bring thousands of sightseers to the locality for the event, and swell the coffers of the tradespeople of the town. Such is human nature.

Chapter XI
The Maloney Mystery

There are times when my friend Sherlock Holmes disappears without notice, and leaves me on my own. My responses to this are not constant. Sometimes, in such an event, I feel deserted and at a loss. There are other times when I welcome the break to get on with aspects of my own life, which perhaps have been neglected.

So it was when I went down to breakfast the following morning to find Holmes's usual chair vacant. At first I was disappointed not to be greeted by my old friend, but presently my spirits lifted with a sense of freedom which surprised me, and with a good breakfast under my belt, I felt indeed as if suddenly I were on holiday.

A holiday was welcome after the excitement of the events into which I had stumbled: the demise of the American Silas Heindecker, with whom by pure chance I had shared a seat on the train from Quebec, and the tragic death in the swamp of the unidentified young man in his well-cut English tweeds. These after all were affairs for Sherlock Holmes, who, as I have observed on more than one occasion, is only truly alive when so challenged.

My mind, I must admit, had returned to the original quest I had undertaken in Canada, which was to locate and report to his family in England the whereabouts and condition of Reggie Braithwaite.

Also, my thoughts were never too far from the enchanting lady Genevieve la Chance. After all, I reasoned, she was my one possible contact in my search for Reggie, and I resolved to again look her up.

I had found her fascinating when we first met on the train, and although she had robbed me of a considerable sum of money, and had surprised me with her circus performance, she was the most interesting female creature I had come across in my travels.

The cold snap had abated, the sun shone, and the remaining leaves were red and gold on the maple trees, in what Canadians term "Indian Summer," so it was with some delight and anticipation that I dressed for the fresh autumn weather and made my way to that charming neighbourhood just north of Bloor Street.

I found the street where the lady resided, and I strolled eastward among young mothers and nursemaids pushing perambulators in the morning sun.

Outside number thirty-four stood a four-horse carriage, a footman up behind. I paused, under pretext of lighting a cigar, behind the sturdy trunk of a nearby maple tree, and in a moment, from the door of the house, came milady. She was dressed as if for travel, in a dove-grey outfit of singular but striking modesty. Her auburn hair was all but concealed beneath a fashionable hat with a dark veil which obscured her lovely features.

Pulling on kid gloves, she was closely followed by the pert Irish maid I had observed on my previous visit, who now called to the coachman to give her a hand with the baggage. It was quite apparent that the lady Genevieve was going away for a few days.

Then a curious thing happened. A hansom cab wheeled in from an adjoining side street, the horse pawing the pavement as it pulled up close to the lady's carriage. From the interior descended a man whose authoritative manner seemed familiar to me. For the moment I could not place him, dressed as he was in top hat and broadcloth, with white linen at his throat. The new arrival paid off his cab, which moved off down the street. He then turned his attention to milady and swept off his hat with a flourish. As she stood there smiling at him, I was consumed with jealousy.

The man replaced his topper at a jaunty angle, and stepping forward, helped the lady into her carriage, in a correct enough manner, I must admit. He then turned to make sure the luggage had been stowed, and it was then that I saw who it was. The bushy walrus moustache had gone. In its place was a handsome set of side whiskers — mutton chops, as they are sometimes termed. But there was no mistaking the cold blue eyes and powerful hands: it was the man I knew as Inspector Maloney of the Schenectady Police.

In one brief moment, luggage stowed to his apparent satisfaction, he climbed into the coach, the footman closed the door and remounted his perch, the driver clucked to his horses, and the vehicle moved off down the street. The Irish maid re-entered the house and closed the door.

Had my friend Sherlock Holmes been there, he probably would have hailed another cab and taken off after the departing vehicle, wherever it was bound. Indeed, I remember him in earlier times on at least one occasion, in hot pursuit, leaping on the back of a cab as it careered through the streets of London.

As it was, I stood for some minutes sucking on my pipe, consumed with jealousy at the aplomb with which my rival, for so I now viewed him, had moved in on milady Genevieve. Was she in danger from this man? Was she in fact herself an agent? Working for whom? Finally I shook off my confusion, and, dodging the baby carriages, made my way to the front door of number thirty-four.

When I am attracted to a member of the opposite sex, I find that her rooms, her home, even her possessions, take on a magic aura of their own. The light seems brighter, the colours more intense. I felt that the ornate door-knocker that I now touched was imbued with such a quality, absurd as it may seem to others. In any event, I lifted the polished brass door-knocker, and gave it a thump. The door opened almost at once, and I was confronted by the Irish maid. She looked at me sharply, intelligence in her dark eyes.

"Doctor Watson?" she said, a question in her voice.

"You remember me, then?"

"I do, sorr," she said, "An' if you're after the mistress, she's just this minute gone."

"Gone?" I said as innocently as I could muster. "Gone where?"

"Niagara Falls. She's in the circus, ye see. But ye'd know that, since it wuz yerself that tended the mistress after her accident."

"I did, Bridget," I said. "The high wire seems a dangerous pastime."

"The mistress has always lived dangerously."

The pert little Bridget offered no more, and I was not adept enough to elicit further confidences.

"Well, thank you very much, Bridget. Perhaps I can find her at the falls," I said.

"Good luck, sorr. I'm sure she'd be pleased to see ye," the girl replied.

I raised my hat to her, and she turned away. The door closed behind her.

Back at the hotel, Sherlock Holmes was nowhere to be found, and as I came down to the lobby again from our rooms, uncertain what to do next, my eye fell upon a poster newly affixed to the hotel notice-board. It was phrased in the extravagant terms reserved for what is termed "show business" on this side of the water:

THE FLAHERTY CIRCUS
PRESENTS
BEAUTIFUL FEMALE FUNAMBULIST
CHALLENGES
THE NIAGARA GORGE
UPON A TIGHTROPE!
SPECIAL WEEKEND EVENT!!

My heart sank within me as I read the document. It was from Niagara that the unfortunate young victim of the swamp murder had come, and it was to Niagara, to the best of my knowledge, that his unknown assailant had returned. It was to Niagara that the lady Genevieve la Chance was now en route to her death-defying performance, walking a tightrope from one shore to the other, high above those turbulent waters!

Niagara Falls, I was to discover, was a centre of entertainment and conviviality, enjoyed by people from both sides of the boundary between Canada and the United Sates. A special event at this location would attract excited crowds in their thousands.

An attempt had been made on the life of Genevieve la Chance on the high wire in Toronto. Why not again at Niagara, before an audience of thousands?

Quickly I packed a small bag, left a note for Holmes, should he return, and, hastening to the railway station, purchased a ticket for Niagara.

". . . baskets on her feet . . ."
(Madame Spelterina)

Chapter XII
The Raging Torrent

I had heard of the custom of this past decade for individuals seeking fame and fortune to challenge the might of Niagara, some by going over the falls in a barrel, to be fished out somewhat battered and bruised a few miles downstream; others by essaying the high wire tightrope across the face of the rushing torrent. Once a Frenchman, Blondin by name, carried a small cookstove with him on the high wire. Halfway across, poised between heaven and earth, he lit the stove and cooked an omelette, lowering half on a string to the little steamboat *Maid of the Mist* which, two hundred feet below, took passengers into the very maw of the raging torrent, and eating the other half himself before continuing on his dangerous way.

Another high wire artiste, Madame Spelterina, danced across with baskets on her feet, surely an inelegant procedure.

But it was such a display of courage, this contest pitting a puny human being against the overwhelming power and indifference of the monumental cataract, that drew thousands of thrill seekers to Niagara Falls. And of course the shills and barkers, the confidence men, were all out to take advantage of such an event. Bets were made upon the very lives of those who placed themselves in such a perilous position over the raging waters. It has even been known for members of the betting fraternity to loosen guy wires, and thus add to the peril of the contender.

Whatever one hears of Niagara Falls, one's first glimpse comes as a shock, the implacable power of the stream rushing over the precipice causing the very ground to shake under one's feet. There is a curious fascination about this never-ending torrent, which attacks the most blasé, acting, they say, as a sexual stimulant. Indeed, the place is advertised as the "Honeymoon Capital of the World," and is very much favoured for that purpose, although, of course, this may be just in the minds of the rascally entrepreneurs.

In any event, in due course I found myself beside this rushing torrent, the unceasing roar of the cataract in my ears, the spray flung high into the blue sky and catching the rays of the sun in arching rainbows. I became aware of the sound of a fife and drum, barely heard above this unceasing rush, as down the crowded esplanade came a motley crew of circus performers.

Brightly dressed clowns did somersaults on the pavement. Red Indians, decked out in eagle feathers and war paint, rode bareback on their spirited ponies, flourishing tomahawks over their heads and uttering sharp war-cries, heightening the sense of danger I felt in the air. Behind the Indians lumbered a ponderous elephant, upon whose back sat Jo-Jo, the little Andaman Islander. He seemed to be enjoying himself, grinning widely and exposing his pointed betel-stained red teeth. Tied to the howdah — the seat on the great beast's back — the little imp had a bunch of bananas, one of which he would tear off from time to time and feed to the elephant, who curled back his trunk to receive the morsel, much to the delight of the crowds who watched the procession pass by.

Then came an open landau, drawn by four spirited horses, top-hatted coachmen up in front. My eye was at once drawn to the three occupants of the vehicle. In the centre, shining like a prima donna, was my lady Genevieve, graciously receiving the accolades of the crowd like a member of royalty.

The other two occupants of the carriage were men. One, his cherubic face beaming with good humour, was Flaherty himself, dressed in hunting pink, with white knee-breeches and a shiny top-hat. The other, smiling, but with restraint, had alert eyes which roved restlessly over the crowd. It was the man I had seen with Genevieve in Toronto. Sleek, dark and sinister to my eye, I could swear it was the American detective Maloney. What his role was, and why he had seen fit to change his appearance, I could only conjecture, assuming that he had been engaged as a bodyguard for the lady Genevieve since the apparent attempt on her life which Holmes and I had witnessed in Toronto.

After the landau came the circus strong-man, clad in his leopard skin and accompanied by his glittering bevy of female acrobats in their abbreviated costumes. Above their heads floated a banner, which gave me a cold shiver of premonition. It read:

"FLAHERTY'S CIRCUS PRESENTS
THE BEAUTIFUL GENEVIEVE LA CHANCE
IN HER DEATH-DEFYING
HIGH WIRE CROSSING OF
NIAGARA FALLS"

I had barely grasped this information when a second elephant came into my view. Upon the beast's great back, riding like a potentate, in a colourful eastern robe, tarbush on head, face darkened, was a familiar figure. My heart leaped with relief, as I recognized the unmistakeable profile. It was, need I say it, my dear friend Sherlock Holmes!

Chapter XIII
A Trap Is Set

The crowd of holiday makers that had descended upon Niagara Falls was almost overwhelming. From town and country within a hundred miles on both sides of the border, they had come, seeking excitement enough to carry them through the long dull months of the coming winter.

One could sense a curious intensity, a brightness of eye, and a loud voice — the kind of thing, the thought occurred to me, that one can observe before a public hanging, and for much the same reason: the thrill of seeing the life of one's fellow human thrown into jeopardy. They had come from far and wide, to see a beautiful young woman challenge the implacable might of Niagara Falls.

I shrugged off the dark thought. In fact, it was a lovely day for the time of year. The sun was shining in the bright autumn sky, and people were having a good time. There was the thrill of donning a mackintosh, and going down wooden steps, under the very falls themselves, to the Cave of the Winds, where the water leaped off the cliff above, and fell in a great and marvellous curtain between the sky and the rock face. Or one could take passage in the little steamboat *Maid of the Mist* and brave the rapids below the falls.

It still being early, I joined the throng strolling along the boulevard, and presently found myself standing in front of Tussaud's Waxworks. Although I was aware of this popular establishment in London, it came as a surprise to see its counterpart here in Niagara Falls. But of course it was a good location for such an enterprise, and very popular judging from the crowds of sightseers entering and leaving the building. I paid the modest entrance fee and went into the building. To a great degree the show resembled what I had seen in London: there was Jack the Ripper, suitably dark and villainous; there was a reproduction of our noble Queen Victoria, with Albert, the Prince Consort, hovering nearby as if awaiting a summons. Then suddenly I was confronted with the effigy of my dear friend Sherlock Holmes, complete with cloak and deerstalker hat, a pipe in his mouth and a magnifying glass in his hand. I was quite taken aback, the effect was so convincing. In fact, to my own embarrassment, I found myself blurting "Holmes?"

The effigy of course paid no attention to my utterance, but one or two people in my vicinity cast me a curious look as they passed by. Recovering, I pressed in to read the text, printed and framed, at the foot of the effigy. It read: "Sherlock Holmes, famous Detective, England. Born January Sixth, 1854. Died Reichenbach Falls, Switzerland, May Eighth, 1891." I realized again how widely mourned was my friend's supposed passage and I wondered what he was now up to.

That evening, I sought out Flaherty's Circus, which had taken shape on the common nearby. Amidst the orderly confusion, with which I was now becoming familiar, I found Sherlock Holmes. This friend of mine, whom I have known for many years, never fails to surprise me. I had seen him assume many guises, perhaps a venerable Italian priest, or an opium addict, but nothing had prepared me for the sight of a dark-faced eastern native, sitting on a mat beside a low table in a circus tent, eating with his fingers from a bowl of curry and mutton.

"Have some cous cous," he said by way of greeting.

"Last time I tried cous cous," I replied, "was in Benares. It made me quite ill."

He peered at me for a moment, then, dipping his fingers into a bowl of water in which floated rose petals, he made a motion towards me reminiscent of a papal blessing. I glanced around. We seemed to have reasonable privacy in our corner of the great tent. In any event, the other members of the troupe were intent on their own affairs. I took out my pocket handkerchief and wiped the drops of rose water from my face.

"What was that about?" I asked uncomfortably, and I sat down beside him.

"Was it not in character?"

Holmes scooped up a handful of boiled cous cous and stuffed it in his mouth.

"Good Lord, Holmes, you do try one's patience at times!" I cried. "As I see it, you have at least three serious problems to solve. And you sit there, flicking rose water in my face!"

"Yes?" He wiped his fingers on the edge of his garment.

"One: who did in Silas Heindecker, the man in the train? Who took his confidential papers? Where are the papers now?"

"Yes?" Holmes took a lump of cous cous in his fingers and molded it into a ball.

"Two: the murder in the swamp. Who did that, and why?"

"And three?"

"Three: what is the role of the lady Genevieve in all this?"

"You appear to be overlooking one of the key players, my dear Watson." He popped the cous cous into his mouth with every sign of satisfaction. "That is the so-called Police Officer Maloney, the undercover agent. Very undercover, I should say. . . ." He broke off; then: "You should really try some of this mutton, Watson. It's terribly good."

I glanced up, catching the hint in Holmes's sudden change of the topic of conversation. Approaching us, threading their way through the groups of performers, past the tethered animals, came two figures, one of whom I recognized as Flaherty, the circus manager. He had changed into his working clothes, flamboyant as ever: knee breeches and riding boots that had seen better days, a garish checked jacket, red and white in colour and a size too big, and his bowler. In his hand he carried a long whip I had seen him use in the ring. With Flaherty was a tall, rather gaunt man wearing his top hat and frock coat with the authority, and indeed the appearance, of Abraham Lincoln himself.

Flaherty's round face wore an air of uncertainty as he approached Holmes, as the latter continued to squat on his grass mat, seemingly detached from this world.

"A-h-h, sorr," said Flaherty uncertainly, trying to attract Holmes's attention. "There's a feller here to see you, sorr."

Holmes made no response, and Flaherty turned to his companion and back again, in some confusion.

"It's the New York Police," said Flaherty. "Inspector Hargreaves."

Holmes looked up from his meditation. "*Salaam, effendi,*" he said, putting his palms together in salutation.

"Good day to you, sir," replied Hargreaves.

"Well, I'll leave you together, then," said Flaherty, and he retreated with alacrity.

Hargreaves sat himself down on a bale of straw, and addressed my friend.

"I have followed your adventures in the past with admiration, Holmes," he said. "And I have always been pleased at our occasional communication. But this manner of meeting, I must say, surpasses anything I had imagined." Our visitor looked around as a camel relieved itself in our vicinity.

Holmes remained in character. "Inspector Hargreaves," he greeted our visitor, "I am most pleased to meet you after all these years. You must forgive this present appearance of a charade."

"I came as quickly as I could after I received your telegram," replied Hargreaves. "Suffice it to say that the fellow Maloney, who represents himself as one of the Schenectady Police Force, acting under my instructions, is a renegade now in the employ of certain international investment houses which have been making fortunes out of what has become known as the 'Canadian Railway Scandals.' The Canadian government experienced difficulty in completing and paying for the gigantic task they had undertaken — their eight-thousand-mile, coast-to-coast railway — and were obliged to borrow a great deal of money."

"Quite," said Holmes.

Holmes had produced a hookah, or water pipe, much favoured in Arab countries, and stuffed its ornate bowl with tobacco. He now applied a match, and in a moment was inhaling the fragrant smoke that bubbled through the rose water.

"I believe there were papers pertaining to this affair," said Holmes, "that one of your government agents was bringing from Britain and Holland for a government signature, before delivering them in Washington. This emissary was found dead in a train leaving Quebec City. The papers were gone."

"Yes. I had a report on that unfortunate incident," replied Hargreaves. "Silas Heindecker, one of the country's best operatives."

"I take it that the papers were incriminating to the unsavory investment houses you mentioned." Holmes blew out a plume of smoke.

"Indeed they were. Evidence strong enough to bring these miscreants to justice."

"Then we had better recover them, had we not?" said Holmes.

"That would be a great service to the governments of at least three nations," said Hargreaves. "Meantime, I must take my man Maloney into custody. I have a warrant for his arrest."

"This fellow — your man as you describe him — I presume is in the pay of the certain unsavory investment houses you have alluded to, and has been given the task of diverting those incriminating papers and seeing that they do not reach the hands of the proper authorities."

"That is correct, Holmes."

"Since, to the best of my knowledge, the man is still here, we must take it that he has not yet succeeded in acquiring the papers. So it follows that if you arrest him now, you will not in fact lay your hands on the papers, since he does not have them."

"True," said Hargreaves.

He looked a little baffled, being lectured by the dark-skinned, robed figure squatting before him. Holmes had returned to his hookah and puffed meditatively upon it, the rose water bubbling in its bowl. His eyes were hooded in that curious way he has. Minutes passed. An elephant nearby trumpeted and shifted its great feet. Closer, I could hear the camel chewing its cud, and somewhere in the great tent, from further away, came the lovely but incongruous sound of a mandolin, playing some popular Italian melody.

Our visitor sat patiently on his bale of straw. Presently he pulled out a case of cigars, opened it, and offered me one. I thanked him and refrained. He lit up and exhaled with an air of satisfaction.

"You know this fellow Maloney personally, of course," said Holmes at last.

"Good Lord, Holmes," replied Hargreaves. "I engaged him in the first place, and approved of his coming up here to Canada! I didn't know how deeply involved he was in what we call 'pay-off.' A rough diamond, I thought him!"

Holmes had reached inside his burnoose, and when his hand reappeared it was clutching a small package wrapped in white tissue paper. He placed it on the low table and removed its wrappings. A random ray of sunlight filtering through the canvas caught the object thus revealed. It was a pair of horn-rimmed spectacles, one lens of which was cracked.

"Spectacles," said Sherlock Holmes.

"Yes, I see that."

"Retrieved from the swamp where a young man was recently done to death."

"The 'Body in the Swamp' murder," observed our visitor. "I had a report on it. The Canadian authorities arrested two drunken pig-butchers for that affair, did they not?"

"They did," replied Holmes. "They were proved innocent of the crime and were released."

Hargreaves directed his gaze to the spectacles as they lay on the table in mute testimony, the cracked lens gleaming in the shifting ray of sunlight.

"What is the significance of the spectacles, may I ask?"

"They did not belong to the victim."

"That's not very useful, Holmes. By all accounts, the place was subsequently swarming with sightseers, any one of whom could have dropped them."

From the sleeve of his flowing burnoose, Holmes extracted three or four envelopes, which he placed on the table before us. With a long brown forefinger he touched them one by one.

"This contains a single human hair, found in the branch of a hawthorn bush, five feet nine inches from the ground, twenty feet from where the body was discovered."

His fingers moved to the second envelope.

"This one contains notes on characteristics of certain footprints found in the mud, under the snow, near the hawthorn bush. Measurements and calculated weight of the individual who made the footprints."

"In the third envelope is a tailor's label, torn from the shirt of the corpse, and trampled into the mud. It enabled me to contact the unfortunate young man's family in London."

"Well, that's something," said Hargreaves.

"This envelope," said Holmes, "contains an eight-millimetre cartridge casing of a Smith and Wesson pistol, recently fired. It was pressed into the mud to a depth of three and one-half inches, by the passage of a heavy man's boot, size 11C, the sole of which had been recently repaired. Autopsy of the deceased, I am told, revealed a bullet of this calibre in the brain."

"Smith and Wesson eight-millimetre is standard issue in the New York Police Department," said our visitor, unhappily.

"Exactly," replied Holmes. "Your man, Inspector."

"You mean — Maloney?"

"I do."

Hargreaves looked grim.

"The victim?"

"An innocent young Englishman of good family, attracted to Canada by promises of a new life in a new land."

"Motive?"

"With an eye to the future, the young man was making enquiries about a particular piece of land that was for sale in the vicinity of Brockville, Ontario, when by mischance his path crossed that of the murderer. I know little more than that, Inspector."

"I must take this man into custody without delay," said Hargreaves, rising.

"May I suggest . . ." said Holmes.

"Yes?" The New York detective sat down again, somewhat impatiently.

"The trap is already set, Hargreaves," said Holmes. "I plan to close it, and deliver the prey into your hands within twenty-four hours. . . ."

"With respect, Holmes, I would just as soon. . . ."

" . . . Along with the stolen document, so important to the case and to your 'governments of at least three nations.'"

Inspector Hargreaves looked at my companion with new respect. He gave him a flinty smile.

"Your argument, Holmes," he said, "is a compelling one. Twenty-four hours, then!"

Chapter XIV
Niagara Falls on a Tightrope

The following morning, at my lodging at the Niagara View Hotel, I was finishing a rather lonely breakfast, pouring a second cup of a rather inferior Assam tea, when I was made aware of a familiar figure sliding into the hitherto empty chair opposite me.

"Good morning, Watson, my dear chap."

It was Sherlock Holmes, his familiar self. My spirits rose.

"Hullo, Holmes. Had breakfast?"

"Yes, I have, actually."

"Cous cous?"

"Bacon and eggs. Quite good."

"What's afoot?"

"Thought you might like to come on a cruise. *Maid of the Mist.*"

"Do I have time for my breakfast this time?"

"I think so. Five minutes."

I groaned. Holmes sat there beaming, stuffing his pipe with the Canadian tobacco to which he had become accustomed. He lit up and exhaled a fragrant cloud of smoke.

"The plot, indeed, does thicken, Watson," he said after a moment. "I don't think I have ever had as many strands coming together at any one time. But they do come together."

". . . in a barrel . . ."
(Carlisle D. Graham)

"I'm glad to hear it, Holmes," I said, mopping up my egg yolk with a piece of toast. "I must admit that I am thoroughly at sea."

A few minutes later, we walked to the boat jetty on the river, below the falls. At this early hour, not too many people were abroad, and we boarded the little steamship *Maid of the Mist* with perhaps ten or a dozen other sightseers. The first mate of the vessel issued each passenger with a mackintosh cape as protection against the spray, as we proceeded closer to the roaring torrent.

Holmes was in a good mood, chatting with the mate and learning the legends of Niagara, from lovelorn Indian maidens who launched themselves over the brink in birch-bark canoes rather than wind up in the arms of the wrong men, to daredevils of today seeking fame and fortune by going over the falls in a barrel.

Above us, presently, we could see the slender wire upon which the lady Genevieve would dance across the maelstrom, in but a few hours' time. Holmes scrutinized the wire with interest. He spoke to the captain of the boat, who obligingly took us closer to the shore, where we could see the anchoring cables of the high wire shackled to cement abutments, thus keeping the wire itself taut above the rapids. Holmes made no comment, but I could not help but recall the agonizing moments of peril when the high wire in the circus tent had come crashing down moments after the performers had slid to safety. Were this to happen here, there could be no escape.

Landing shortly, we made our way, at Holmes's suggestion, to the waxworks, where at this early hour we were the only visitors. Standing in front of his own wax effigy, Sherlock Holmes smiled gently.

"Such is fame, Watson. A wax image!"

"You say it comes together, Holmes," I ventured, as we left the waxworks.

"Do you not see it, dear chap?"

"I can't say that I do," I replied.

Preparations were being made for the day's events, and expectations were raised to their highest. Tomorrow, the crowds would disperse and return to their hamlets and farms to face the challenge of the long northern winter. Flaherty's circus would cross the Canada-U.S. border for the winter circuit in the more hospitable climes of Florida and the southern states.

In the gathering crowd, Holmes and I walked down the street together towards the fairgrounds. "Consider the sequence of events," said he. "In Quebec City, Watson, as you board the train, you are accosted by a beautiful woman in distress — "

"Accosted, Holmes?" I exclaimed.

"Precisely," replied my companion. "It is a well-known observation amongst confidence tricksters, that individuals in transit, in an environment strange to them, are more vulnerable than those on their home turf. That is why railway stations, steamboats and the like are a favourite haunt of such rascals, male and female, who prey upon the innocent traveller."

"You are suggesting that the lady took me for a dupe!" I said.

"I do indeed, my dear Watson," replied Holmes, bluntly. "She passed to you money that proved to be stolen, did she not?"

"Yes, but — "

"She eluded her gentleman friend, who in all innocence had come to join her on the train. That gentleman subsequently was found dead, robbed of sensitive papers of considerable political importance."

"Surely you are not suggesting — "

"By implicating you with stolen money, and contriving to have her friend die in your company, suspicion was thrown upon you, Watson, very efficiently, I might say, while the lady walked away without blemish. May I remind you, my dear fellow, that it was you who landed in Kingston Gaol, unable to give a convincing account of yourself."

"And may I remind you, dear Holmes," said I somewhat nettled at his observations, "that while the so-called murder was being committed, you were in the next carriage but one!"

"Quite," said my friend shortly.

We threaded our way through the expectant crowd towards the circus quarters, and the individual caravans that seemingly housed the performers when they were not travelling.

"I must tell you, Watson," said my friend, after a few moments, "as you may have noted in our years of association, I am not always infallible. Particularly where beautiful women are concerned!"

I glanced at Holmes, touched by his admission, and warmed by his confidence in me.

As we entered the circus quarters I sensed an air of expectation. Costumed performers, clowns, Red Indians, animal handlers were collecting in the vicinity of the gaily painted caravans. Flaherty, self-important in fresh white riding breeches and his best top hat, pushed through the crowd, his blue eyes gleaming with good cheer. He mounted the steps of one of the caravans, and turned to the assembly. A trumpet sounded, and a drum rattled.

"Attention, everybody!" Flaherty's voice, trained in the clamour of the Midway, rose above the buzz of conversation from the crowd. "Today is our last big show in Canada this season. Tomorrow we pack up, bag and baggage, and move across the border to the warmer climes of Florida for the winter months. I want to thank you all for the past season, and to wish you well for the next."

There was applause at this announcement, and Flaherty, a rotund figure in his red coat, held up his hands again. The crowd quieted.

"And now," he proclaimed, "I want you to give special applause to the beautiful and talented star of our show, one who is loved and admired by all, who this afternoon will thrill thousands with her death-defying crossing of Niagara Falls on a tightrope."

The trumpet gave vent to a veritable cascade of notes, the door of the caravan opened, and the crowd burst into a storm of cheers. My own heart, dare I admit it, skipped a beat, for there, poised, framed in the door of the ornately decorated gypsy caravan, was Genevieve, radiant and shining, a veritable goddess being paid tribute by lesser mortals. Gone was the discreet grey tailored suiting, the veils, and the fashionable Paris hat. Instead, a brief acrobatic costume, shimmering with sequins, displayed her divine figure. Her dark hair was swept back, and jewels glittered in her shapely ears. She had the most slender waist I had ever seen. Her eyes shone with delight at being so welcomed by her associates, and perhaps with the heightened consciousness of her coming ordeal.

Through the crowd came an elephant, painted and decorated as if for a Hindu wedding. Upon its back was a palanquin of embroidered silk, within which colourful cushions had been placed for the comfort of its occupant. Straddling the neck of the great beast, in white turban and robe, solemn with his responsibility, rode Jo-Jo the pygmy.

The crowd parted as the great animal moved into position before the caravan, so that the lady Genevieve could more easily gain access to the palanquin. This she now did, moving with agility and grace, to the applause of the admiring throng, a rattle of kettledrums, and a discordant blast of trumpets. The elephant, with its precious cargo, then moved ponderously out, escorted by the Red Indians with their flowing eagle feathers, the somersaulting clowns, and the animals. The circus enclosure was left virtually empty, save for one or two maintenance men at a distance, and Jo-Jo's little monkey, who sat happily on a packing case, eating a banana.

I was about to follow the parade when I was aware of a movement in the caravan so recently vacated by the lady Genevieve. I paused in mid-stride, and waited for I knew not what.

The doorknob twisted under an unseen hand, and, strangely, I felt the hairs prickle on my neck. Slowly the door swung open, and there in the opening stood the dapper figure of Inspector Maloney.

When I had last seen the fellow, he was in a four-horse carriage escorting Genevieve, the lady to whom I had lost my heart, and I had been consumed with jealousy. As I saw him now, emerging from the intimacy of her boudoir, I was overcome with a sudden violent rage, and without thought I rushed to attack him physically. It was not only that he was a rival for the affections of the lady, it was also the knowledge of the perfidy of the man, who in pursuit of his own gain had committed the most heinous of crimes.

I know how to use my fists in a pinch, and I was able to give him a thorough trouncing, he being taken unawares. Suffice it to say that, at my sudden attack, the slender black moroccan-leather briefcase that he was carrying flew out of his hands and was at once snatched up by Jo-Jo's little monkey. It was then that Sherlock Holmes and Inspector Hargreaves appeared and clapped handcuffs on the miscreant, Hargreaves intoning the appropriate legal terms of arrest.

The monkey, chattering with excitement, had retreated, and now observed the scene from a safe distance, clutching the leather case in one hairy hand.

Holmes shot me a glance of frustration. In our long association, I had rarely known him to fail to wrap up a case neatly and economically. Here, however, because of my intervention, he had in fact delivered the miscreant to justice, as promised, but the important papers, which could be a major embarrassment to three nations, were in the hands of an agile monkey, gibbering and grimacing at us, beyond our immediate reach.

"Thank you, Holmes," said Hargreaves. "I am taking this fellow in charge. I leave it to you to retrieve the documents."

So saying, the New York detective hustled his prisoner out of the enclosure. Holmes and I watched them go, then Holmes turned to me.

"Thank you, Watson, for your timely assistance," he said coldly.

"Right you are, Holmes," said I, feeling a fool, but refusing to reveal it or to apologize.

I mean, dash it all, it was bound to happen sooner or later. Although Holmes has invited me to attend his cases for years, he has almost invariably kept the important elements of a given investigation to himself, until he chose to reveal them. It was no fault of mine that he had not taken me earlier into his confidence on this occasion.

"How the devil do we catch that monkey?" asked Holmes.

"He's fond of bananas," I replied.

Holmes looked over the scene with a cold eye — the animal cages, the tiger showing its teeth in a silent snarl.

"There's a bunch of bananas over there," he said, pointing to the empty elephant stall.

"Right," I said, and promptly made myself useful by crossing to the indicated spot.

I had gained the elephant stall and reached up to the bunch of bananas to break off a couple of the riper ones, when I felt a soft "plop!" on the back of my collar.

Instantly there was an urgent cry from Holmes. "Don't move, Watson! For your life!"

There are moments when perhaps, dare I say it, I regret having met Holmes at all, all those years ago. This was one. But perhaps it is unfair of me to blame my good friend for the predicaments I constantly find myself sharing with him.

I opened my mouth to ask him why I should not move, but as I did so, I was conscious of a tickling sensation which moved from my neck across my jaw to my cheek. There it rested, and I closed my mouth again carefully.

I was aware of Holmes, who had now moved swiftly and silently to the front of the tiger's cage. I saw what he was after. It was the long whip that Flaherty used in the ring to guide his animals through their performances.

I squinted sideways, obliquely, down my cheek, and saw in my distorted vision a large brown spider. Vivid in my memory was the crumpled figure in the train of the unfortunate Silas Heindecker, and the laconic announcement in the Kingston *Whig Standard* of finding in the deceased man's luggage a large brown spider of unknown, "presumably tropical," species.

Holmes had retrieved the whip, and the tiger growled softly, watching as my friend silently approached me, his eyes focussed intently upon the horrific creature on my face. In a moment, Holmes's arm came up, and the lash snaked towards me. I felt its passage in the air and the whip cracked with explosive force beside my cheek. The horror which had been sitting there was gone!

"Are you all right, Watson?" queried Sherlock Holmes, setting aside the whip.

"Yes. Thank you, Holmes," I said, fingering my cheek.

The spider lay on the floor at my feet, inert, split open by the force of the whiplash.

"What a beastly creature," I said.

"Yes. An arachnid, if I am not mistaken, of a particularly virulent type." Holmes, with his insatiable curiosity, was kneeling beside the dead horror, examining it through his magnifying glass. "If modern methods of transportation expand to bring in foodstuffs, particularly bananas, from foreign places, they are going to have to find some way of eliminating such creatures before delivery to an unsuspecting public. Perhaps some form of fumigation of the railway boxcars." He was thoughtful for a moment, as if making a mental note of the matter. Then he rose to his feet and restored the glass to his pocket. "Now, where the devil is that confounded monkey?" said Holmes. He reached up and broke off a banana.

At that moment Jo-Jo's little simian reappeared, having been scared away by Holmes' action with the whip. He was still clutching the precious dispatch case in one hairy hand.

"Aha, there he is!" said my companion. He held out the banana. "Here, my fine fellow!"

But the little beast was wary and kept his distance, his bright eyes moving from Holmes to myself and back again.

"Try peeling the banana, Holmes. He might find it more appealing," I offered.

The monkey watched Holmes's precise motions in removing the skin from the banana, and indeed came closer, the better to see the action. But when my friend then held the naked fruit towards him, the creature was seized with sudden suspicion. He backed away, his lips curling, curiously reminiscent of Jo-Jo, his master. I wondered for a moment about the singular relationship between man and monkey, when suddenly the little beast took off towards the door.

"Seize him, Watson!" cried Holmes.

I attempted to do so, and was promptly smothered by the hairy creature, arms, legs and snarling visage, and try as I would to contain him, he slipped out of my arms, leaving, for my pains, a pungent odour in my nostrils, and a tuft of reddish brown hair in my fingers.

"Confound the beast!" exclaimed Holmes. His eye lighted on the bit of fur clasped in my fingers, and in a moment, from his pocket, he produced one of the envelopes with which he travelled.

"Pop it in there, would you Watson?"

"What?" I replied.

"The confounded bit of hair in your fingers!"

"Oh, yes."

I did as he requested, and he crammed the envelope back in his pocket, making a beeline for the open door through which the monkey had departed. On gaining the open air, we glimpsed the creature scurrying away from us down the crowded pavement, lugging the briefcase half as big as himself. In a moment, finding the growing crowds too restrictive, he took to the trees which lined the esplanade, and was now happily swinging from branch to branch in pursuit of the drums we could hear in the distance.

Holmes, I could see, was annoyed. I could recall a few times in our long association when he had been outwitted by his opponent, once incidentally by a woman, but to be out-maneuvered by a gibbering monkey was, I suspect, more than his pride could bear. I, on the other hand, was more concerned with the safety of the lady Genevieve. It was no secret that sizeable wagers were being placed on the success of her imminent high-wire performance, by the thousands of people who had thronged in to watch the spectacle. How long would she take to negotiate the slender wire from Canada to America. Whether she would wear baskets on her feet as the late Madame Spelterina had done. Whether she would walk, or dance, non-stop across the chasm, or pause in mid-flight, as it were, poised over the maelstrom betwixt heaven and earth, and present some surprising element of histrionics to thrill her audience. Whether, in fact, she would make it at all!

Still sharp in my mind was the "accident" in Flaherty's circus tent, which sent the whole high wire contraption crashing down moments after Genevieve and her fellow performers had scrambled to safety.

Pushing our way vigorously through the throng, Holmes and I got close enough to the parade to see the great elephant moving ponderously through the excited crowd, the palanquin swaying on its back, and the lady Genevieve throwing kisses from within her silken bower. Seated cross-legged on the elephant's neck rode Jo-Jo the pygmy, his dark eyes as much on his mistress as they were on the road ahead of him, and, as we got closer, it came to me in that moment, that the diminutive creature from an unknown culture half a world away had lost his savage heart, even as I had, to this cultured, beautiful western woman.

"Can you see that confounded monkey?" barked Sherlock Holmes.

Chapter XV
The Further Shore

Apprehensive as I was for the safety of Genevieve, there was little I could do. Along with thousands of other onlookers, I watched as she was attended by her cherubic manager Flaherty, with his red coat and shiny top hat. To a roll of kettledrums she descended from the back of the elephant and mounted a low platform decorated with flags and banners which had been erected at the Canadian end of the high wire. The wire stretched taut and shining to the further shore.

Damp with spray, a balancing pole caught and reflected the rays of the sun, as milady took it up and held it horizontally between her slender hands. The crowd became silent, and the roar of the falls seemed to grow louder, as if to overwhelm the slender creature who so courageously challenged its might.

The roll of the drums ceased. The lady paused for a moment, then with every appearance of confidence she stepped onto the taut wire, and without further hesitation walked gracefully, poised on air, towards the centre of the span. In the blown spray, shining in the sun, a series of small rainbows appeared, as if conjured up by the show business acumen of Flaherty, who at this moment mounted the platform, arms raised in salutation. The crowd roared its approval.

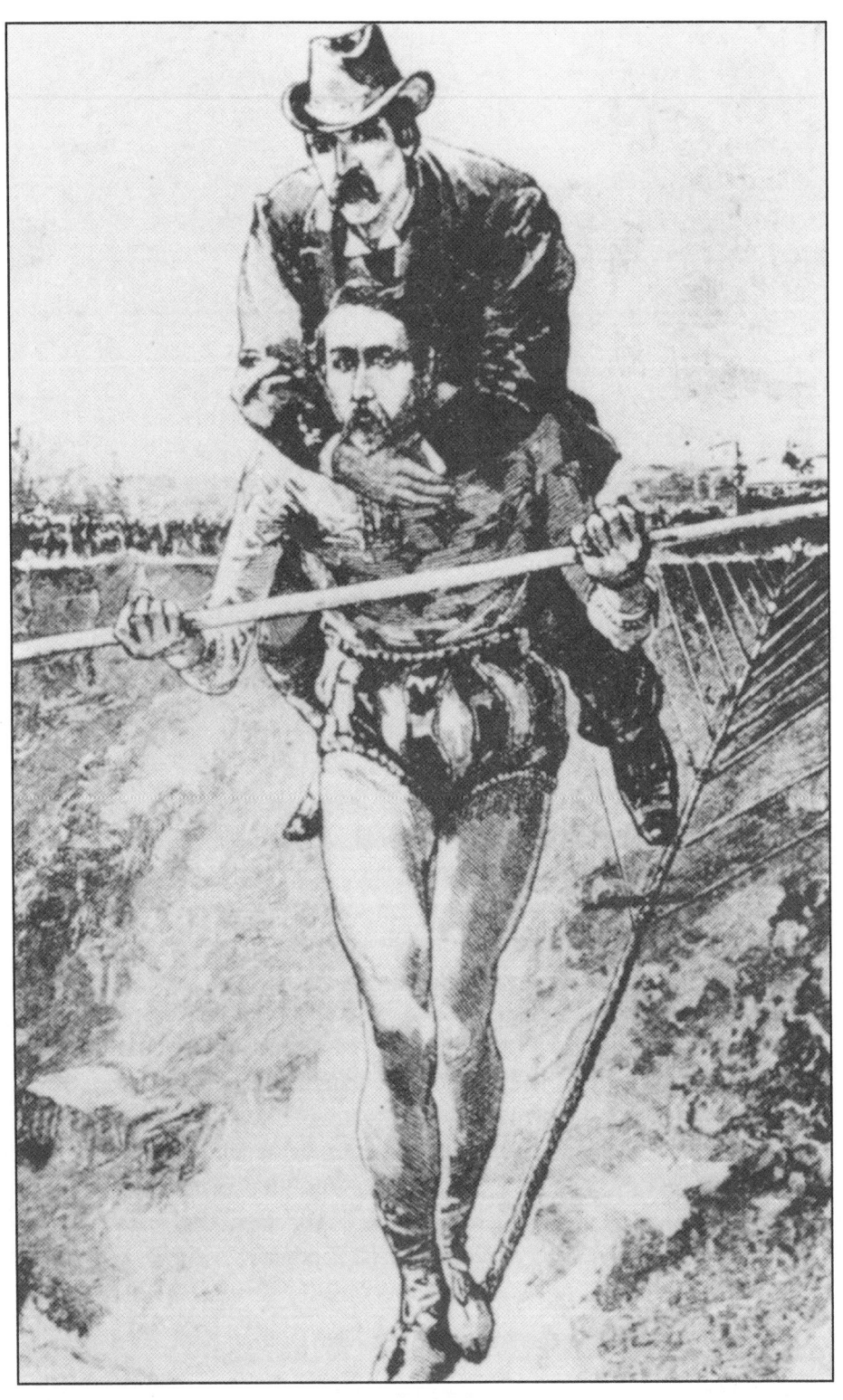

". . . manipulating the balance pole. . . "

I watched the lady's progress with growing apprehension, for I felt that whoever had caused the high wire accident in Flaherty's circus tent would not fail to try again, but the wire remained as taut as a violin string, and the lady moved upon it with utter grace and confidence.

The halfway point was marked by a red flag, which fluttered in the aerial turbulence occasioned by the falling water. Reaching this mark, the shining figure paused in mid-flight, and turning around to face her audience, she executed a graceful arabesque upon the slender wire. The crowd again shouted its approval, and the lady curtsied in elegant recognition.

Then with infinite grace and daring, manipulating the balance pole, she stood on her hands on the steel wire and slowly rotated her slender body a full circle over the horrendous rapids, before regaining her original position.

The throng renewed its tumultuous applause, and in reply the lady reached down and untied the red flag from the wire at her feet. She straightened up and waved the flag over her head, as if in salutation.

Then a curious thing occurred. As if awaiting her signal, Jo-Jo the Andaman Islander slid from the back of his elephant and, mounting the platform, ran without hesitation directly out onto the wire, his bare toes gripping the steel cable. Upon his shoulder was the monkey, and clutched in the hand of the monkey I could see the black leather diplomatic pouch that contained the stolen papers, whose disclosure threatened the peace of three nations.

Jo-Jo and the monkey joined the lady at the centre of the wire, where the pygmy turned and directed his wide, betel-nut, sharp-toothed grin towards the shore. The crowd broke into renewed and delighted applause at this embellishment of the high wire performance. The lady smiled and curtsied, and the monkey displayed its teeth in a wide grimace, holding aloft the bag of documents. Then, turning, all three of them crossed to the other side, disappearing into the curtain of mist and shifting rainbows that marked the American shore.

Holmes's face was a study in frustration.

"I shall never understand women," he said.

Holmes and I walked back through the dwindling crowd away from the falls. Engineers were already dismantling the apparatus that controlled the tension on the high wire. We watched for a minute.

"Holmes," I said. "After the close call in the circus tent, I must say I feared the worst here in Niagara."

"That is why these fellows are here, Watson," Holmes was cryptic in his response. "Each is an agent, forewarned of such an eventuality. As to the circus-tent affair, I am glad to say that the perpetrator of that foul deed is in custody." My friend's voice was sharp, concealing his present frustration. "It was Maloney, intent on getting his hands on the papers, and eliminating his arch-rival at the same time."

"His arch-rival?"

"The lady Genevieve."

We were interrupted by the Lincoln-esque figure of Inspector Hargreaves, who approached us smiling, his hands outstretched in greeting.

"My dear Holmes," he said. "May I congratulate you!"

Holmes turned to the newcomer. "Are congratulations in order, Hargreaves?"

"Forever modest, eh, Holmes?" our visitor chuckled warmly. "I am directed by the President of the United States to present you with his compliments," he said. "And with this invitation to attend him in the White House as his personal guest."

Hargreaves fished an embossed envelope from an inner pocket and pressed it upon Holmes.

"At your earliest convenience," he added. "I think he may have some international matters of some moment, on which to seek your advice."

"Ah," said Holmes. "The lady Genevieve is well then, I take it?"

"Yes, indeed. She is sitting in a private railway coach just across the bridge, sent for her convenience and safe passage to Washington. She was sipping a glass of champagne when I left."

"And — the papers?" asked Holmes.

"The papers? Safe and sound, thanks to your astute and imaginative handling of the matter."

"Ah, good," nodded Holmes, modestly.

Chapter XVI
The Matter Is Resolved

Holmes and I were on our way back to the waxworks museum. "There is just one thing I want to clear up to my satisfaction," said my friend.

"What's that?" I asked.

"Who, or what, killed the American agent Heindecker — under my very nose," he added with chagrin.

We turned into the building we sought. The crowds were dwindling, and we had the place to ourselves. Sunlight streamed through the windows and cast flickering light and shadow over the waxen figures, imparting to them a semblance of life. General Brock, gallant and bemedalled, again led the assault on Queenston Heights. The Royal Consort Albert stood awaiting the command of Her Regal Majesty Victoria, and the figure of Holmes, pipe in mouth, sat with his head bent in thought over his deal table, which was stained and marked with his chemical experiments and littered with test tubes and Bunsen burners.

"I thought so," he cried.

"What's that, Holmes?" I queried.

"A comparison microscope."

So saying, Holmes moved in beside his counterpart, giving me a curious sensation of double vision.

With a familiarity born of years of practice, he drew the microscope towards him and removed the dust cap. "Quite a good make. It appears to be in good condition," he stated, and forthwith took from his pocket the last two of his envelopes. Using tweezers, from one envelope he retrieved the single hair he had so painstakingly recovered from the seat of the train, where I had first met the lady Genevieve. From the other envelope he took the tuft of hair that had been left in my hand after my ineffective grappling with Jo-Jo's monkey.

Holmes then deftly prepared the two slides for a comparison test and slid them under the microscope. He peered into the eyepiece and made a slight adjustment to the lenses.

"Eureka," he said quietly, and stood aside for me to look.

Viewed through the powerful magnifying lenses of the comparative microscope, the hairs were identical.

"From which we may conjecture, Watson, that while you were in the dining room of the train, Heindecker was having his own quiet dinner in his seat; a bottle of wine, and half a roast chicken. Somewhere during the proceedings, the door into the adjoining carriage opened a few inches, the monkey quietly entered, and, unseen by Heindecker, dropped the virulent arachnid into his open Gladstone bag. Heindecker reached into the bag, and the spider bit him. Voila!"

"The marks of the spider were on Heindecker's throat, Holmes," I stated. "Not on his hand."

"That's a small thing, Watson."

"My dear Holmes," said I, with some restraint," I have heard you say more than once that little things can be of infinite importance."

"Well, then, Watson," replied Holmes, with some acerbity, "may I now say that there is an exception to every rule?"

"What was the motive, then?" I asked.

"The motive was to retrieve for the lady Genevieve the briefcase that Heindecker had purloined, containing incriminating evidence affecting the future of three governments."

"Surely it wasn't necessary to drop a deadly spider into the man's baggage to achieve that," I cried.

"You were closer to the event than I was, my dear chap. What is your version?"

"I think the papers were incidental," I said. "I think it was love. I believe that little Jo-Jo, the Andaman Islander, worshipped the lady Genevieve from afar, as they say. I believe that their association started long before I arrived on the scene, and when Jo-Jo discovered that Heindecker was the cause of the lady's misfortunes, in his primitive mind he simply thought to do the fellow in, using the means to hand, namely the deadly spider with which he was quite familiar."

"What about the wine?" said Holmes.

"The wine?" I said. "The fellow should have been more careful in selecting his vintage."

Holmes glanced at me for a moment, surprised perhaps at my blunt and outspoken language. He was about to say more, I thought, but instead glanced at his pocket watch.

"Do forgive me, Watson, dear chap. I really must get my things together. I have an important appointment in Washington."

Together we entered our hotel and checked at the desk for keys to our rooms. "Doctor Watson, sir," cried the young man behind the counter. "There is a telegram for you."

He handed over the missive, which I opened with curiosity. Who would be sending me telegrams in this faraway land? It was from Hartford Manor, Kent, the home of my old medical associate Braithwaite, whose wayward son I had been ineffectually pursuing.

It read: "Reggie joined NWMP believed Regina. Wd. still apprec. news. Regards."

I showed the telegram to Holmes.

"Northwest Mounted Police, Regina," he mused. "That's pretty much the Canadian frontier, is it not? Point of departure for the far north. Are there not rumours of gold in those parts?"

"So I understand, Holmes."

"Are you going?"

"I thought I might . . . you being otherwise engaged, as it were."

Holmes folded the telegram in his long fingers.

"The far north!" He allowed me one of his rare smiles and handed me back the telegram. "From all accounts it could prove quite interesting." His eyes gleamed as he spoke.

"Yes, I hope so," said I.

Holmes paused a moment, and then said, "Look here, Watson. After I have finished this business in Washington, could we not join forces in this northern enterprise?"

"My dear fellow!" I responded warmly. "Nothing could please me more!"